it's all about Jack!

Marel Brady

it's all about Jack!

TATE PUBLISHING

AND ENTERPRISES, LLC

It's All About Jack!
Copyright © 2012 by Marel Brady. All rights reserved.

Published by Tate Publishing & Enterprises, LLC
127 E. Trade Center Terrace | Mustang, Oklahoma 73064 USA
1.888.361.9473 | www.tatepublishing.com

Tate Publishing is committed to excellence in the publishing industry. The company reflects the philosophy established by the founders, based on Psalm 68:11,

"The Lord gave the word and great was the company of those who published it."

Book design copyright © 2012 by Tate Publishing, LLC. All rights reserved.
Cover design by Kenna Davis
Interior design by Errol Villamante
Published in the United States of America

ISBN: 978-1-62024-344-2
1. Fiction / Romance / Suspense
2. Fiction / General
12.07.17

Grace 1

Jack looked splendid as he left for the office this morning: his first day as Chairman of Spelectra. The months of excitement, persuading business associates to invest in this new technology, are over. Spelectra will transform the solar energy industry! My misgivings over Jack using our retirement nest egg seem to be unfounded. After twenty-five years as a devoted husband and father, Jack now has the freedom to follow his dreams. Jessica and Edward surprised me; they were all for it. "Go for it, Dad," was their advice, but then young people seem to have no fears. I guess they've got nothing to lose and think they'll live forever. Now it looks like I was wrong. Yesterday the *Washington Post* published a favorable article about the start-up, so the future looks rosy. I'm so glad Jack's office is closer to home. Tyson's Corner is an ideal spot; maybe I'll have lunch with him, sometimes, and do some shopping in the Galleria afterward. I suppose those are my dreams…to spend more time with Jack and lead a more leisurely life, but that's been pushed into the future, yet again. I'll just have to be patient.

Hiring staff hasn't been easy for Jack. I mean, who wants to take this kind of risk? Jack was particularly disappointed that

Kendra didn't join his new venture. It seems there are limits to his powers of persuasion! I can't blame her. Why would she give up a secure position to throw in her lot with Jack? She has years of service with the company and three children to think about.

So…a new start for Jack…and a huge void for me. I felt needed and wanted, helping Jack, while all the initial negotiations were underway. It was exciting to be part of the action. Now, I'll have to content myself with snippets of gossip over dinner. I wonder what his new assistant will be like? Better than me, that's for sure! These young people are so into technology, and they're all highly qualified. I'll miss the mental stimulation, but I'll just have to find something else to sink my teeth into. I suppose I'll need to pick up with all my previous activities. It's all going to seem tame in comparison.

I need to get out of my pajamas now and get cracking. I must admit, I've enjoyed the leisurely morning, but I need to get action orientated. I'll make some phone calls this afternoon and get my life going again. Have to give that some thought while I'm in the shower. Who should I phone first?

Kendra 1

I'm dreading today! My first day with the new boss! Will the good impression be accurate, or will he be a monster? I'm the one who'll be the first to know! He's very different from Jack. The senior staff thought he was very personable when he dropped by to make his introductions a few weeks ago. I thought so, too, but only time will tell. It's been weird not having a proper boss these last few months. It's been difficult to replace Jack, I suppose; he did give plenty of notice of his intentions, but I guess it takes time to find the right person to replace him.

I keep wondering if I did the right thing, turning down Jack's offer to join his new venture. But it's all too scary. Alternative energy is all very new. It could be a huge flop or a huge success. I just can't take that kind of risk. I'm not sure how I would fit into that scene anyway. The place will probably be full of younger people, wearing jeans.

Anyway, I should be making lunch boxes for the kids. But there's plenty of time. Getting to sleep has been difficult these past few weeks. Anxiety, I suppose. This temporary place is not ideal. Waking up in the early hours of the morning is taking a toll on me. Perhaps, after today, I might feel better. Once I get over the first day with the new boss.

So what am I going to put in the lunch boxes today? I just can't afford to pay for school lunches; I don't think they're very nutritious anyway. I've got that huge pineapple, which was a special deal at the grocery store. I'll cut that into chunks. But then they need protein, so I think I'll make cheese sandwiches. I need to make sure the kids are well fed, but I need to keep a close watch on our finances, too.

This economy is frightening. They're calling it the Great Recession now! I'm not just hearing about job losses on the television. I'm hearing about friends who've been laid off, right here in Virginia. I'm concerned about my own job security. I just don't know what the future holds. I'll need to think about upgrading my skills. If I don't get along with the new boss, I'll have to reconsider my situation. Right now, I don't see any other position in the company that would be right for me. I'll have to work hard at making a success of this relationship with the new guy. I'll have to make myself indispensible. I'll have to make myself look good today. I'll need to look well groomed. I'll need to be smiling and relaxed. Oh, dear!

Grace 2

I need to take Jack's shirts to the laundry today. I noticed he has some red wine stains on his new shirt. He really is drinking too much. He returned from the office last night looking a little weary. I scold him all the time about not looking after himself properly; he just doesn't do what the doctor tells him. After his heart attack last year, he needs to lose weight and exercise, but business always takes priority over his health. There's no point in me worrying. Well, I do really. I'm anxious all the time, and it manifests itself into constant scolding. Occasionally, he gets mad at being treated like a schoolboy. But what can you do with a man who doesn't look after himself and who almost died recently? Edward scolds him too, but why would a man take his son's advice when he pays no heed to his wife?

I also need to get tags for my car. I got quite a fright when a man knocked on my window at the traffic lights yesterday as he was crossing the road. He yelled out that my tags had expired. True enough, they're eight months out of date. I don't know how I managed to let that slip. Too many distractions with Jack's new venture, that's what's happened.

I haven't been sleeping well these last few nights. My neck and throat are painful, the soles of my feet are burning, and I have pins and needles in my legs. I can ignore the pain during the day, but at night, the discomfort keeps me awake. Weird symptoms, really… I can't think what might be causing this…maybe a virus. I just hope it goes away soon.

I'm looking forward to the weekend. We have two farewell parties to attend. Miriam is organizing a party for one of our neighbors whose husband lost his job. They're really shocked and will have to return to Texas. Her spirits are at rock bottom, so it won't be too much of a fun occasion. The other will be a festive occasion, an intimate potluck dinner for twelve people. The hostess goes to so much trouble whenever she extends an invitation to her home. Her husband has a big promotion, and they're transferring to California, so everyone will be in high spirits. Maybe I should have organized a party to celebrate the start of Jack's new company, but it seems a little premature; after, all it might not be a success. Better to wait and see the results, I think.

Kendra 2

Living without a proper home is sucking the energy out of me! I feel so weary! This rental place is nice enough, but the landlord is difficult. I've been paying the rent on time every month and keeping the place in meticulous condition, but whenever there are any repairs needing done, he's always slow to react and penny-pinching with the contractors. The lease expires at the end of the month, but the rent has been increased, and I can't afford to pay more. Moving out into a temporary place while I look for another rental property will be a huge upheaval for the children, but there's nothing else I can do. I can't ask for a pay rise in these difficult times. So, I have to allow the place to be viewed by possible new tenants, which means having strangers tramping through the place. I was hoping that with the rent increase, there wouldn't be many viewings; thankfully that's what happened.

We haven't been disturbed until now, but last night, while I was trying to make dinner, there were two agents showing a client around. I really thought the viewing would only take half an hour, but they were here for a whole hour. I just had a phone call a few minutes ago to say that someone else wants to see the place tonight, so we'll be disturbed again. I just have to hope the agents sign him up so I'll get peace until we move out.

Tomorrow I'll have to start packing all our belongings. I've got some old boxes from the office in the back of the car and loads of newspaper, so that'll be the fun activity for the children tonight. I'm hoping Stanley can help out during the weekend. I can get so much done if he takes the kids for the whole day. I really should divorce him, but as long as we're still legally married, his healthcare plan is still good for me and the kids. I really should transfer to the healthcare plan at work, but Stanley's cover is better for all of us. He's not such a bad guy, really. Sometimes, he's quite sweet, and I feel a pang of remorse at putting the whole family through this separation. But the arguments were foul and too distressing for the kids. We've just grown apart. He says I became a snob when I started working for Jack. That's a joke! I was more like the poor kid, with my nose pressed up against the window pane. It was a whole new world seeing how people like Jack live.

I just wish I had a good future for myself and my children. I can't stop thinking about it. Jack and Grace have been married for twenty-five years, and they just got back from a big celebration on a fabulous yacht in the Caribbean. How I wish I could enjoy their lifestyle! I'm so jealous! They travel first class everywhere. They own a wonderful home. They're financially secure. I wish I could live like that, but there's only one way to achieve what I want. I need to find a man.

Grace 3

I so wanted to go to the Cherry Blossom
Festival in DC at the weekend. Jack knew it was on because
it was mentioned in the office, but he said we'll give it a miss
because the weather forecast is rain. Every year we intend to
make it to the festival, but every year, something gets in the way.
I find it fascinating that the festival originates from the emperor
of Japan gifting thirty-five thousand cherry trees to the president
of the United States in 1912. By 1935, the trees were mature
and looking wonderful, so the festival was inaugurated. Halfway
through our aimless Saturday, Jack suggested we go to the festival.
I don't know whether he was bored or feeling guilty; however, it
would be no fun in bad weather, so I opted to give it a miss.
Perhaps we'll make it next year.

I looked in the mirror today and was shocked to notice wrinkles
on my earlobes. I can't imagine how this happened. I guess it's the
price of decades of sunscreen on the face and forgetting the ears.
I tried to think whether my grandmother had wrinkles on her
earlobes, but it's not a thing you tend to notice in detail. I'll have
to pay particular attention to all my friends now. They'll think I've
gone crazy, staring at their ears. I guess we're all getting older. It's

getting harder to look nice these days. I should put in more effort. After all, there are lots of attractive young women out there.

Today, Jack is in Los Angeles on business; he's inspecting the new manufacturing facility. I packed his bag to perfection. I can get two suits, five shirts and ties, a pair of shoes, and everything else he needs for a five-day trip into a case that fits into an aircraft overhead locker. Jack always looks nice. I always worry whenever he visits California. This time, they're having storms that closed the freeways. I was anxious that his flights might be delayed, but he just phoned to say everything was on schedule. He says evidence of the economic downturn is everywhere, noticeable even at the Trump Golf Course in Palos Verdes, where he played with two, potentially, major clients. He says he paved the way for some new business under brilliant sunshine, after the stormy weather had passed, but they were one of the few groups on the course. Capturing sunshine is what Jack's new business is all about, so the weather played into his hands. It's so exciting to think that his revolutionary design of solar panels could change the world economy!

Jack mentioned that he's concerned about the welfare of Kendra, who is struggling financially. Apparently, he heard, through the grapevine, that she's having a tough time. I do feel sorry for her. One of her daughters is called Tiramisu. I can hardly believe that someone would be named after an Italian dessert. I think it's quite irresponsible! Apparently, as soon as Kendra laid eyes on her daughter, she declared her to be her favorite sweet thing. The family has some Italian heritage; the nickname became temporary until the christening, but that morning, Kendra decided to keep the name; she calls her Su for short. I wonder if she really is a sweet thing. Jessica was such a sweet thing when she was a little girl...the adorable daughter I always wanted. I do hope Kendra can keep her family in good shape. It's not easy being a single parent.

Kendra 3

Well, there is some justice in the world! The landlord is due for a hefty plumbing bill, as well as loss of rent. We have water escaping between the walls, which will have to be cut open to solve the problem. Already you can smell the mold, so that's another expensive problem for the landlord to solve. The repair will take a while and can't be done until we move out because the fumes from the mold are toxic. I just hope the spores from the mold haven't gotten into our clothes. As the plumber said, it's a good time to move out. We had to rip out a chunk of carpet that was wet and causing nasty smells, so this looks really bad whenever prospective tenants are viewing. They can see the foundation slab has cracked due to saturation. So it looks like it'll be some time before the landlord gets another tenant. No sympathy from me!

In the meantime, I'm keeping the water turned off as much as possible, which is really difficult with three kids, but they're amazing. Any change of routine seems to fill them with excitement. What stresses me out is great fun for them. They're taking turns running outside and turning off the water. The responsibility makes them feel really grown up. I'm just delighted this activity is causing such fun since it's bitterly cold outside.

I got a lot done last night. My plan is to pack our suitcases with as many clothes as possible. What doesn't fit in the suitcases will have to go into boxes. One of the gals in the office has a truck and has offered to help me out. I think I'll accept her kindness since I don't think I can face the hostility from Stanley. He's very moody right now; the bad economy is hurting him, too. Once we get into the temporary apartment, we'll be living out of suitcases. I just hope the children find this a fun activity, too. Once we're out of here, I'll make contact with some agents and look for advertisements in the newspapers.

Moving is so time consuming! I don't even have time for a haircut! Yesterday, I took the children to a barber's shop and got all three done for thirty bucks. Watching the hairdresser and thinking that I'm racing against the clock with this house move, I decided to take the plunge and let the barber loose on my hair. My thought was ...what the heck...let's go really short so it lasts a long time...it can't be too bad...it'll grow out. Well, surprise, surprise! In fifteen minutes, he had me shorn, and it's hideous! What was I thinking? I wonder if my new boss will notice.

Grace 4

I've been housebound for the last two days, mostly doing chores and paperwork, so I enjoyed coffee at a friend's home in Langley Oaks today—a good excuse to dress in smart clothes instead of my comfortable house attire. My friend is a charming French lady, so needless to say, all the goodies were mouth-watering. However, I need to lose a few pounds to get into a dress in a few weeks' time, so I enjoyed the savory items and steered clear of the sweet things. It's hard to get rid of vanity! Some of the ladies wanted to go for lunch afterward, so I joined them at the McLean Family Restaurant in Salona Village. I gazed at the faces of my friends, etching their features into my memory: kind, smiling, wonderful people who make my life worthwhile. It was a pleasant morning, although I don't feel as if I achieved anything.

After lunch, I needed to have a new battery in my watch. I do need to be able to tell the time, even though I'm not doing much. I had to go away out to Herndon because the local watchmaker is on vacation. Driving back home, those strange symptoms started up again—burning sensation on the soles of my feet, tingling in my legs, numbness in my throat, burning on my tongue, tenderness on my skull, swelling on my gums, my neck felt strangled, and my breathing was shallow. I stopped in a driveway and used my cell phone to call the doctor; he immediately fitted me in between patients. Nothing showed up on the examination. My lungs are clear, and there's no infection on my throat. I asked the doctor for clues as to what all these symptoms might mean, but he just said it could be a virus.

Jack knows I've been having these strange symptoms recently. I don't know why I didn't tell him about seeing the doctor. He didn't ask about my day, so I just kept quiet. Part of me feels resentful and part of me doesn't want to worry him. Maybe I kept quiet because he's going on about Kendra again.

Apparently, she has some maintenance issues in her apartment. I was irritated, but I tried to be understanding. I do feel sorry for Kendra. I just don't know how she survives on her salary with three children and married to that Stanley, who is lazy and earns very little. I suppose she was young and foolish. Her accommodation situation is not ideal. Jack tells me she was woken up on Saturday morning by banging noises outside her apartment, which went on for hours because the maintenance team was replacing boards on the building due to termite damage. Jack asked me to think about helping her out somehow. I don't know what he expects me to do about Kendra's problems.

Sometimes it feels like all I hear about is how much Jack misses Kendra, how hard she used to work, how energetic she is, how much initiative she displays, what a great sense of humor she has. I'm tired of hearing about all her woes. I know it's all been a rough transition for her, and money seems to be an issue, but you do have to work at a marriage. Perhaps if she had put in some more effort, she might still be under the same roof as Stanley, without all these worries. One of Jack's suggestions is that we pay for her removal costs. I said nothing; this might have been a generous gesture, in the past. Now, with our retirement fund invested in the new venture, the idea seems quite reckless. I don't know what other crazy ideas he's got up his sleeve!

Kendra 4

The moving saga continues! I requested a property inspection so there are no shocks on the big day. Yesterday, the landlord sent around agents who glanced at everything, said "Beautiful, honey," and offered me a handshake. They had come totally unprepared without a copy of the move-out document and refused to sign that I would get my deposit back! I told them their lack of professionalism was appalling. One of the agents countered that he "used to think I was a nice person" and flounced out to another appointment. The other agent stayed behind and agreed to sign a separate document confirming that my full deposit would be refunded without any deductions. A few hours later, the agent who had flounced out made the pretext of needing to accompany a viewing in order to enter the property. When he arrived, he was alone, saying the appointment had been cancelled. He agreed the property was in immaculate condition, gave me a signed copy of the move-out document, and stated he didn't want any bad feelings. The next thing, he was giving me a hug, asking to be friends again. I bet he wished he hadn't given me a hug since I hadn't showered and my clothes weren't too fresh due to the plumbing problems.

I don't trust those agents one bit. I won't feel comfortable until I get my deposit back. What a savior Jack is in all this muddle! He knows the problems we've been having with the plumbing and the difficulty in packing and transporting our stuff. I was knocked out when he called to say that he and Grace would pay for professional movers as an advance housewarming present for our new place. I was completely astounded. It gave me goose bumps, and the tears flowed. I just managed to blurt out, "Thank you," and had to end the call. I couldn't bring myself to tell Jack that I've got some cash in the bank, thanks to my split from Stanley.

It's been hard dragging myself to work every day. It just feels like a huge weight has lifted off my shoulders now. I'm feeling much more relaxed. Now I'll be able to focus on giving my new boss the professional assistance he deserves. We've not established much of a relationship yet. He's been out of the office a lot, spending his time meeting all the staff.

Grace 5

Well, we made it to the Cherry Blossom Festival in glorious weather yesterday. After breakfast, we donned our walking shoes and took the Metro from Dun Loring into DC. We weren't sure where to get off, but the train was jammed with day-trippers who advised that Smithsonian was the best stop. It seemed like everyone in the world was headed for the cherry blossoms. The whole area was thronged with people, many wearing summer clothes since the temperature was tipped to reach seventy degrees. Truly, it was like a summer's day.

We made our way toward the Washington Monument, following the crowds up the National Mall. Many families were picnicking in the sun, so it really was a holiday atmosphere. We started our day with a visit to the World War II Memorial, a tribute to the fifty million souls who perished. The atmosphere was quiet and reflective. We viewed the memorial and gave silent thanks to our forbears who fought for our freedom.

Lured away by our search for cherry blossoms, we made our way toward a pink line in the distance. We were rewarded by the sight of the Tidal Basin ringed in blossoms, all in full bloom. Somehow, it seemed imperative to walk the entire circuit, not to miss a single tree. I'm not sure of the distance around the perimeter, but it must be several miles. Crowds of people, of all nationalities, were strolling under the pink blossom umbrellas, many taking photographs while creating chaos among the pedestrian traffic along the narrow pathway. Halfway along our circuit, we sat on the steps of the Thomas Jefferson Memorial to rest our weary legs. Jack was all right, but I was exhausted.

After paying our respects at the memorial, we were in desperate need of refreshment. We trudged all the way back up the Mall to the Smithsonian Castle in the hope of finding comfortable surroundings for a light lunch. My feet were so sore, and my legs were aching. I could hardly make it up the steps of the building. A pleasant but exhausting day out!

I need to work on getting Jack on another excursion. He did moan quite a lot, complaining that one cherry blossom tree looks just like another! He was annoyed that we couldn't even get a decent lunch, after all that exercise, since the café at the Smithsonian had run out of food, but he did use it as a good excuse to have a few glasses of wine.

Today, I'm suffering from such an ambitious sojourn. The tingling in my hands and feet is scary, and I've been losing my balance around the house. I feel really exhausted…almost like I have flu but without the sniffles. I can hardly drag myself around. I need to make another appointment with the doctor. I can't believe this is just a virus.

Kendra 5

Yesterday was awful! My new boss summoned me into his office to tell me off about a glitch in his meeting schedule. He told me he wanted to have a serious discussion with me; then he told me I seemed to be sulking rather than taking the feedback on board. Then he said he couldn't have an assistant building up a bad attitude, that he's the boss and I have to get things right, and that he can't have standards slipping. I just wanted to cry. I managed to mutter an apology and just left his office. Jack would never treat me in this way!

I'm an emotional wreck right now! It's been a challenging twenty-four hours. This morning, the moving company arrived on the scene. The guys were really nice—two brothers who packed everything neatly away; at least they tried to, until they ran out of boxes and had to go to U-haul to buy more. Of course, we have no running water, so the guys had to give me advance warning of needing a comfort break so the water could be turned on temporarily. I bought doughnuts for the guys first thing in the morning, so that was the start of a good relationship. I was hoping one of the brothers would fancy me and ask me for a date. Just for my self-esteem, if nothing else. The guy who owns the truck is married. It's a great shame because he's really cute. Normally, his wife travels with him to do the paperwork, but business is in the tank right now. She has taken a job preparing food in a hotel kitchen to help pay the bills. The other brother is single. He's kinda cute with a great physique. I flirted with him, but he didn't respond, so that didn't do much for my ego. While the guys were here, the television was blaring out details of tent cities springing up all around the country. So many people have lost their jobs and their homes that there's no room in the homeless shelters. These are good, decent people, not vagrants—nice men and women who are reduced to these terrible circumstances.

By late afternoon, everything was packed away, so I decided to burn some personal papers. I did think of taking them into the office to put through the shredder, but there was such a lot that I decided to burn them in a huge planter on the patio. Suddenly, the next door neighbor was hanging over the fence, shouting and yelling at me! He does shout a lot. We can hear him arguing with his wife all the time. There was just a little smoke wisping up, but he yelled that he was calling the fire brigade. Next thing I know, within a few minutes, there are two policeman banging at the door, four firemen rush inside the house, and there's a huge fire engine parked outside! The guys were so nice and told me I wasn't in any trouble. I told them this guy next door has a dog that barks all day long, but I never complain about that. They told me I should contact the animal control department. These guys were so cute! They took a note of my name and phone number. After they left, I allowed myself to dream that one of them called to ask me for a date. My fantasy world where everything starts to come right! I just can't wait to get out of this place now!

Grace 6

The housekeeper comes tomorrow, so I've been making everything tidy. Yesterday, I stacked all Jack's magazines in a neat pile instead of lying open at the pages he was in the middle of reading. He got very annoyed. To smooth the waters while he was watching television in the family room, I made a cup of coffee for each of us, with two cookies on the saucer. When I wasn't looking, Jack hid one of my cookies but told me he had eaten it. I was incensed! I left the room in a temper, but I cooled down quickly and then saw the funny side. I went back into the room with the whole packet of cookies and started throwing them at Jack. He picked the cookies up and threw them back. Before I knew it, there were cookie crumbs everywhere—on the carpet, on the sofa, on the drapes, in our hair, and all over our clothes. There's no way I would have done this if the house wasn't getting cleaned tomorrow.

I need to get Jack initiated into maintenance and catering. He has no idea how to look after himself. I need to, somehow, get him to come with me to the grocery stores and understand all the maintenance in the house, but he's always so tired. He just came back from New York. He took the train this time. He says it's quicker than flying, just under three hours on the Acela from Union Station. I did ask if I could accompany him on this trip, but it never seems to work out; there's always some reason. Anyway, I just don't feel like I have the energy for traveling. The swimming pool was drained for the winter, and I want to be here when the pool guy comes to get it ready for the summer. Jack says I'm making a fuss about all this maintenance, but somebody has to do it. He just doesn't seem to understand anything, unless it's about business.

Kendra 6

Well, we made it to the temporary apartment in McLean! Stanley arrived in a van, late as usual, after not responding to all my frantic phone calls during the day! By the time we reached the apartment complex, it was dark and the administration office was closed. We had to get into the place using instructions on a lock box, and Stanley disappeared without a care in the world. I was crushed. The place was really cold, we couldn't find our pajamas, and the toilet overflowed. Thankfully, there was a plunger in the apartment, so we managed to unblock the toilet. Without pajamas, all we could do was go straight to bed wearing our clothes. The kids were just fine. They're so calm and relaxed under pressure. Any change of routine is exciting for them. We all slept badly. I didn't anticipate the noise level on International Drive would be so bad. The location is great for the malls at Tyson's, but the traffic noise is really loud. Huge trucks roar past in the middle of the night and seem to feel the need to rev up their engines at the traffic light just outside our window!

Next morning, my spirits were low. Daylight showed the carpets in the apartment were badly stained, and the walls were covered in dirty marks. I decided to find breakfast somewhere and bundled the kids into the car. The nearest place I could find was the Westpark Hotel. It was really comforting to enter somewhere warm and clean. We gorged ourselves on the buffet breakfast and enjoyed relaxing in the pleasant surroundings. The next mission was to find somewhere to buy groceries. We went to the Harris Teeter store nearby. Unbelievable! Everything was displayed beautifully, and there were lots of free samples, which kept the kids amused. We stocked up with all the essentials and had fun creating lunch from the vast array in the salad bar. Of course, the kids chose all the wrong things, like chocolate pudding, but discipline has to go on hold for the moment. The kids' excitement at the whole change of environment and routine keeps my spirits buoyant.

Returning to the apartment, I used the emergency number to report the faulty heating. We had to stay put until the maintenance man arrived, which took two hours. He replaced the thermostat but informed us that the whole system was useless! The hot water and the heating are combined. You can use one or the other but not both at the same time, so we need to switch off the heating to take a shower. My contract on this apartment is for two months. I felt so despondent that I sat down on the edge of the bed, and the tears flowed. I'll have to start searching for another place to live on Monday.

Grace 7

I feel like a useless person. The kids don't need me anymore. They have their own lives. Jack could easily survive without me. I don't work. My days are spent mostly alone at home, doing chores or paperwork. It doesn't matter what I wear. My most practical outfit is a pair of jeans, an old tee shirt, and comfortable shoes. Wallet, keys, and phone fit in the pockets of the jeans; the old tee shirt copes with household stains; the comfortable shoes take me all over the house, out to the mailbox, into the car, around to the anonymous grocery store, back to the garage, and return me to yet another long spell of isolation to prepare dinner. The hours disappear as I wonder what time Jack might come home from the office.

Occasionally, I turn into a butterfly. Yesterday was one of those days. Fitting my life around Jack's business requirements has meant avoiding commitments in order to be available to help him pack for trips, or be ready to provide a dinner party at a moment's notice for his business associates. Yesterday, however, was a special occasion at the golf club, so I put my name down weeks ago and looked forward, with some delight and trepidation, to the event. (Trepidation because my golf game has been sadly

29

neglected for quite some time due to my health issues, and delight to be wearing something special and anticipating lunch with a bunch of truly wonderful women.) I so enjoyed the day but was stunned to learn that one of our members has lost her son. He took his own life. Several years of battling with Lyme's disease had proved too much to bear. He swallowed several pints of antifreeze and went out wandering into the woodlands where he first contracted the condition, almost as if he offered himself up as a sacrifice to the quirks of nature that had first altered his life, allowing himself to be attacked by insects, birds, coyotes, bears, and any other predators in the wilds.

Lyme's disease is a terrible affliction. One bite by a tick and your life is altered forever. This young man took his life at twenty years old. He was first taken to the doctor when he was fourteen, after being bitten by a tick when searching in rough grass for a lost golf ball. A two-week course of antibiotics seemed to be the end of the matter. Five years after being bitten by the tick, the young man became severely ill with headaches and muscle pain; eventually, he lost his hearing, had trouble processing information, and couldn't walk. The affliction took over the lives of his family, who spent all their time and energy battling with insurance companies to cover the massive cost of treatments. Losing most of his friends, watching the devastating effect on his family, and being condemned to a life of pain and isolation, the young man eventually took a course of action that would free everyone from the situation. The symptoms of Lyme's disease are very similar to the symptoms of multiple sclerosis. Hearing about all of this has worried me greatly. All the odd symptoms I've been having are similar to Lyme's disease. I need to phone the doctor's office, first thing in the morning.

Kendra 7

I'm feeling frustrated now! I spent the last three weeks looking at houses, and nothing fits the bill. This apartment is not in a state of good repair! I took this morning off work to be here for the maintenance people. The refrigerator isn't working, the lights at the front door are flickering, the hot water comes and goes, the washing machine makes loud screaming noises when filling with water, and the fan from the heating system turns itself on in the middle of the night, also making lots of noise. The maintenance crew is very nice. The boss is a grandmother from Peru, a squat little woman with amazing strength who managed to move the refrigerator all on her own. She worked for two hours on the refrigerator, which was totally blocked with frozen water, but then she discovered the fan and the water valve needed to be replaced. The electrician fixed a faulty connection on the lights, replaced a valve in the hot water heater that was affecting the flow of hot water, and worked on the relay of the heating system. By this time, it was well past lunch, and they still had some work to do, so they disappeared, leaving me in the apartment, waiting for them to return.

I called the office to give my new boss an update, but he told me to stay home until all the work was completed. He was very abrupt! Jack wouldn't have been like that at all! I feel really guilty because there were several conference calls and meetings today with some very important people, so one of the other secretaries would need to step into my place. Getting someone to substitute for me causes so much aggravation. It's like a favor system. I don't want to get behind.

When the kids came home from school, I just had to get out of the apartment. I decided we needed a little treat, so I took them to Harris Teeter to buy one of their fresh pizzas. The pizzas are wonderful. They're absolutely huge, and you can have several varieties of toppings all in one pizza. We took our meal through to the coffee area and demolished the lot very quickly.

Tomorrow is secretary's day. I remember, last year, when Jack took me to lunch at Café Renaissance in Vienna for secretary's day. I thought it might feel a little uncomfortable just the two of us, but Jack is such a nice man that I ended up telling him my life story. I do miss seeing him at work. Grace is so lucky to be married to such a wonderful man! Lots of women in my situation would be looking for a man, and I need to give that a lot of thought. Maybe I should invest in some online dating agency. If the right man came along, it would make life a lot less difficult. I wouldn't have to work. I could stay home with the kids, and their education and health care would be provided. I suppose this is a just a pipe dream. I just have to stay positive!

Grace 8

Yesterday was secretary's day. Jack took his new secretary out to lunch; he doesn't say much about her. Last year, when he took Kendra out to lunch, he bought a new tie for the occasion. I did wonder about that, but she's not in his life anymore. He has never bought a new tie to take me out to lunch; in fact, he never takes me to lunch.

I'm really looking forward to the weekend. Can't wait to see Jessica! I want to hear all about her new job. She seems to like Boston and has no inclination to return to Virginia; she says she would rather suffer a Boston winter than a Virginia summer. I don't know where she gets these ideas. Anyway, this visit isn't to spend time with me and Jack but to attend the wedding of a school friend. Jessica is so focused on throwing herself into life; she has no idea how much I feel a gaping hole in my heart when she's not around. We're taking her to a concert at Wolf Trap this evening. I've been putting a picnic together, but the weather forecast is not good. I've been packing rain jackets and umbrellas. Jack tells me I'm fussing too much.

Each time we see Jessica, she's less like the daughter we once knew. Her life seems to be totally geared around work. Sometimes, she works all night; these accounting firms really get their pound of flesh out of their junior staff. When she's not working, she's exercising at the gym or drinking with her colleagues. I'm worried. She seems to have dropped most of her relationships from the past. I'm concerned that she might be binge drinking; that's what these young people do. They work hard and play hard, without giving a thought to the longer-term repercussions. I just hope she can stay on the straight and narrow.

Jack is picking Jessica up at the airport this evening on his way home from the office. Last night, I asked him to have a gentle word with her about her lifestyle…a good opportunity when they're in the car together. He says any advice will fall on deaf ears. I wonder if he'll dodge the issue. Last time she was here, she told us that she doesn't ever want to get married and have children; the focus of her life will be on her career. She's a headstrong girl and may just hold onto these convictions. She doesn't say so, but I'm sure if she met the right man, she would change her mind. She tells us that if she ever did marry, she would choose an older man who would support her career. It all seems like a defense mechanism for having no love in her life.

I hope Jack's mood improves with Jessica's visit; he tells me I'm treating him like a schoolboy. I try to look after him, but he tells me I'm too controlling, that I'm scolding him all the time. I'll have to be on my best behavior when Jessica's here.

Kendra 8

Well, my budget is looking better every day! Watching rental values online for properties that I already viewed, I can see that asking prices are being reduced all the time. It doesn't seem like I need to rush into anything. I'll just keep looking until the best deal comes along.

I've been coughing so much recently. I just don't know what's causing this. My throat and my tongue are burning. At night, it takes me hours to get to sleep because the coughing is so bad. I got some over the counter stuff at the pharmacy, so I hope I'll get some sleep tonight. In front of me in line was a middle-aged man who was asked to pay over two hundred dollars as a co-pay on his prescription. He was very shocked and told the assistant he didn't have the money to pay. Before I knew what I was doing, I stepped forward and said, "Put it on my credit card." Maybe I'll have second thoughts when the bill comes in, but to see the look of relief on that man's face was worth every cent.

Su took her driver's test yesterday. I can hardly believe that my little girl is old enough to drive a car! My heart was in my mouth as we made our way to the DMV on Gallows Road. Neither of us spoke on the whole journey. The tension level was very high.

She was in a pissy mood last night, screaming and yelling for no good reason, but that's teenagers. I kept my head down and allowed her to let off steam. But I wouldn't tolerate that kind of behavior normally.

Anyway, you never know what kind of examiner you'll get, so my nails were digging into the palms of my hand as I hoped for a kind-looking face to call her name. Thankfully, a softly spoken middle-aged man escorted her out of the side door to the parking lot. It was all I could do not to follow them and drive behind to make sure everything was all right. Well, she passed! She came back into the crowded office with a great big grin on her face, which she had to control for the photograph. We were both so relieved that we hugged and kissed each other. So my eldest daughter is now queen of the road! Of course, the next problem will be her wanting to have her own car. This would be just fantastic, but I can't go spending my nest egg on another vehicle.

However, we did have a little celebration. I took her to the Silver Diner for breakfast. We both had wonderful crab cakes topped with poached eggs, followed by huge milkshakes. It was the best I've felt in weeks!

Grace 9

Jessica's visit was such a joy. Wanting to give her a little treat, I made appointments for us at the Queen & King Salon on Old Dominion Drive. We spent a lovely afternoon having manicures and pedicures by these delightfully delicate creatures from Vietnam. The girls all chatter to each other in a singsong voice while working on their clients. I have no idea what they're saying, but it all sounds very lighthearted. I couldn't believe the state of Jessica's feet; all that exercising in gymnasiums as well as wearing high heels all day long has taken a toll—another testament to the lifestyle of a young professional. Well, she was so thrilled with the pedicure; there seemed to be no treatment that was not lavished on her; she was walking on air toward her manicurist.

Jessica's visit lifted my spirits, so when choosing a nail color, I decided to be really silly. After all, I'm not going to a wedding. I have nothing important in my life this week. So, much to Jessica's amusement, I chose bright green. Not content with that, I got glittery stripes painted on top; we were both giggling like schoolgirls as we left the salon.

I'm feeling downhearted now that Jessica is gone; her visit makes me realize how empty our lives are without the children. Jessica phoned to say thank you for a nice weekend; she says she loves that her bedroom is just the way she left it when she went to college; she loves to reflect on her life in the surroundings of her teenage years. You never know what you're going to get next from Jessica. But she's entirely independent. I don't know what she's doing on a daily basis in Boston, so I just have to put it out of my mind.

The tingling in my hands and my feet has been bothering me again today. I lost my balance at one point during the weekend, just as Jessica was leaving. I was standing by the fireplace when she came over to give me a farewell hug. As she came toward me, I almost toppled over. Thankfully, I could put my hand up to the mantelpiece to save myself from crashing down. I'm feeling exhausted right now. I'm trying to hold on to all the good feelings of Jessica's visit.

I didn't tell Jack that I went to see a neurologist on Friday. He's very preoccupied with the new venture. Lots of new contracts are coming in; he's exuberant and full of energy. I don't want to burden him with my medical problems and spoil all his high spirits. It was good to put health issues out of my mind for a few days. The neurologist tested me for hours—my reflexes, my coordination, my balance, my hearing, and my eyesight. He wants me to go for an MRI scan. I pressed him to give me possible causes for my symptoms, but he couldn't comment. He just said there was a range of possibilities, maybe even a virus. I've been checking all these symptoms on the Internet. I just wonder if I could have multiple sclerosis or Lyme's disease, or even a brain tumor; the symptoms are similar. Self-diagnosis on the Internet is really scary. I discovered that multiple sclerosis is damage to the central nervous system, the brain and the spinal cord. The prognosis is terrifying! The best thing to do is grit my teeth, carry on with my daily life, and confront the issue further down the tracks.

Kendra 9

As my feet hit the floor on Saturday morning, I could feel the carpet was wet! I had to call the maintenance people, who agreed to send someone around before noon. Water leaks are treated as an emergency, so instead of making for the great outdoors, we were marooned in the apartment all morning. It now seems that the malfunctioning refrigerator has been quietly leaking over a wide area. The apartment looks a real mess now. The linoleum tiles are all ripped up in the kitchen area, the carpets are all torn up in the hallway, and we have noisy dehumidifiers drying out the flooring. I bet this water leak has been the cause of my coughing all the time. It only takes a little dampness and twenty-four hours to produce mold in our humid Virginia climate.

So we just couldn't wait to make our way to Great Falls Park on Sunday. What a picnic we put together: cold ham; a salad with apples, walnuts, and raisins; and chocolate brownies all washed down with mango juice. It was quite healthy really. After we had eaten and the younger two had run themselves ragged playing with a friendly Labrador dog belonging to another family of visitors, we decided to walk on our favorite River Trail. The children all know to be very careful where they put their hands and feet on this trail. I've never seen any of those poisonous Copperhead snakes, but they do inhabit the rocks in the area. We admired the spectacular views of the falls before setting off on our hike. No matter how many times I see that view, I never cease to be amazed at the vastness of the scene. Such a contrast to our tiny apartment. We were in such high spirits by late afternoon. The children were scrambling over the huge rocks like billy goats and were smiling and greeting families who passed us on the trail. My thoughts were to be thankful for such a great facility in our area and to be pleased that we were all getting fresh air and exercise.

Suddenly, there was a shout! Su's voice, well ahead, gave a loud yell and then silence. I couldn't see her anywhere. Scrambling over rocks to see what was going on, I found her lying on her back. She was yelling that she had broken her leg. She said she heard a crack when she fell and just knew that's what she had done. I tried my cell phone, but there was no signal, and I was panicking until I saw two young men approaching us. Thankfully, they managed to carry Su back to the visitor's center. Very quickly, an ambulance arrived to take us to Fairfax Hospital. Unfortunately, we were in rush hour traffic by this time, so a journey that should have taken fifteen minutes took nearly an hour. What a bummer! Our little family was so carefree and in such high spirits just a little earlier in the day.

Grace 10

One of the toilets is out of commission and the front door lock needs replacing, so I had to stay home all morning to allow entry to the maintenance people. Never mind…it gave me time to read the newspapers and work out a menu. We have some of Jack's business associates coming for dinner tomorrow, so I need to browse through the recipe books and get out to the grocery store. I think I'll do smoked salmon pate served with champagne, followed by beef bourguignon along with wild rice, asparagus sprinkled with parmesan, carrots coated in honey mustard, and fresh fruit salad for dessert.

I can't wait for this long summer to end; all my activities just die away for two months. I've been amusing myself in the basement for the past week. I think back to my summer art class, last year… I don't know how I managed to produce so many paintings. It really was a feather in my cap that I sold most of them at the McLean art festival. I just don't have the energy to stand for long painting sessions, right now. This morning, I cleared out the basement and took a fancy to producing art from abandoned objects… I feel like an abandoned object, myself, right now. I changed my mind when a flyer in the mailbox announced that a charity would collect unwanted bric-a-brac from the doorstep next week. Perhaps someone else can make use of my abandoned objects and I can get out of the house more often.

I really envy people who go out to work. I know they have a lot of responsibility, but they're out there in the workplace, using their brains in a stimulating environment; they have a reason to dress smartly and be out among other people every day and come home to be needed by their children. I wish I had a salary that I earned myself. I'm very lucky, yet I do wish I could do something useful. Nobody needs me anymore. I need to be doing something that makes me feel valued; my role at home is useful, I suppose, but it's just not enough.

Maybe Jack is right. He says I'm suffering from empty-nest syndrome... I guess I am lonely with not enough to do. Jack says every little minor thing irritates me, and I'm always scolding him. He says he wants to buy me a dog to keep me company; he talked about some breeds for me to consider—maybe a Tibetan Terrier or a King Charles Spaniel. I would prefer a rescue dog, but I'm not sure if it's a good idea to tie myself down—a dog would keep me at home even more. Perhaps I'll ask around, make a few phone calls, and check out some breeds.

Kendra 10

Su is being such a little brat! She was so looking forward to the weeks ahead. Jack had organized a little job for her in the company mailroom over spring break. It would have worked out so well. But she can't work now because the job needs someone who can walk around the building. So the company found someone else to take her place. Jack would have found her a little desk job, I'm sure! So instead of earning money and learning a little bit about the workplace, Su is now hobbling around the apartment on crutches. She's not able to do anything for herself. She can't wash herself or dress herself. All I can do is leave her at home all day. I arranged for one or two friends to drop by and check that she's okay, but she's like a caged animal in the apartment. This morning, we had to visit the specialist to make sure her leg was mending properly. It really was a battle to get her into the car. It's just so awkward on crutches. It really makes me have empathy with anyone who is handicapped.

Anyway, we got to the doctor's office, and I asked if there was a wheelchair. Well, Su went off the deep end, shouting and yelling that she didn't need a wheelchair. She threw the crutches at me, which, thankfully, missed and hit the wall behind. The receptionist and the other patients looked on wide-eyed at the behavior of a belligerent teenager. They just don't understand how difficult it has been for her. She's bitterly disappointed at losing her job over spring break and frustrated at the lack of privacy and independence. It just manifests itself in anger. It was all very embarrassing! I just kept cool and didn't say a word. I knew she would calm down quickly. I think back to my own teenage years…wasted on Stanley. I wasn't much older than Su when we got married. I hope Su makes better choices with her life!

So time is slipping by. What's in front of us is a bunch of medical bills. We do have good health insurance, thanks to Stanley, but there's a co-pay of thirty dollars each time. I dread the day that all the bills hit, emergency room charges amounting to over a thousand dollars, and I have to pay half of that! It's taking such a lot of time to deal with all the paperwork. Well, there's no use in whining! I just have keep up the daily battle of survival. What does worry me is that Su has started some kind of relationship with one of those young men who helped carry her out of Great Falls Park. They've been chatting on the phone quite a lot. My main concern is that he's a lot older. I don't want her led astray by some stranger.

Grace 11

On Saturday, I persuaded Jack to go shopping; he could do with some more casual shoes. After mooching around the designer shops at the Galleria, with no success, we drove to Tyson's, looking forward to a quick lunch at Seasons 52, before trekking to the shoe department in Nordstrom. It took an eternity to get parked; we ended up on the top level and had to walk to the entrance in the rain. I stayed on the top floor of the complex since I wanted to browse around the home wares department at Macy's. I still dream that, someday, Jessica will get married and I will be planning her wedding, so I like to drool over all the china and crystal, but, of course, I never buy anything. On our way back home, we noticed signs for a Middle East food festival at a church on Lewinsville Road. Opening the doors of the car, we were assailed with Middle Eastern music. At the entrance to the church, a young man in white-and-gold vestments directed us to enter the church for vespers and a tour of the church. We've never been to vespers, so we had no idea what to expect. Our church attendance has always been confined to weddings and funerals. Well, it was quite entertaining; there was lots of singing and chanting, lots of holy men wearing embroidered vestments, lots of incense and jingling bells. Truly, it was a bit like watching a Gilbert & Sullivan performance of the Mikado. Afterward, a tour of the church and the baptistery was quite interesting, but what impressed me most was the energy and devotion of the young man in the white-and-gold vestments. He believes that baptism and following Christ allows followers to escape death because they're always ready to be rejoined with their maker in heaven—certainly a concept that gives food for thought. The festival and church tour goes on over the whole weekend as a fundraiser. I estimated the event would bring in at least twenty thousand dollars, but Jack placed a bet with me that the figure would be four times my estimate since the church was filled to capacity, and the hall was seething with people. I must drop by next weekend and pick up their newsletter. I really want to see if Jack's estimate is close to the mark.

So Saturday was quite a good day being out and about with Jack, but I'm not feeling too well today. I was terribly, terribly ill on Sunday. I've never experienced anything like it. I woke up around four o'clock in the morning with awful pains and spent the next few hours vomiting again and again and again. Jack was so sympathetic. He hates to see me unwell. He made me cups of chamomile tea all day while he got no breakfast or lunch. We were invited to some friends for a barbeque, but there was no way I could make it, so I persuaded Jack to go alone. I couldn't possibly cook a meal, so he was going to have to starve or find a takeaway place. So off he went to the barbeque, looking very lonely and perplexed. He didn't stay long, but at least he got something to eat. This morning, I wasn't fit to make breakfast for him; he said he would pick something up on the way to the office. I feel so useless!

Some time today, I need to summon up the energy to make an appointment for an MRI scan. The doctor called, and we had a long discussion about the results from the neurologist. I'm really scared now! The scan will be a horrible experience, and then I have to sweat waiting for the results. I'll be stuck into a tube and kept there for a long time while all the technology scans my body; it's amazing from a diagnostic point of view, I suppose. The doctor says it can be a very claustrophobic experience... I can ask for soothing music to be played, or I can take a sedative. He's sending a prescription in the mail. I haven't told Jack any of this; he doesn't know about the neurologist or anything. I don't want to worry him when he's got so much on his plate with the new business.

Kendra 11

Yesterday, I came home from work to find Su reading a little red book! It turns out that one of her friends who was visiting gave her some interesting literature to read. I'm happy to see her reading rather than slumped in front of the TV, but once she limped off to bed with her crutches, I realized this little red book was actually *The Thoughts of Chairman Mao*. I'll have to tackle her about this in the morning. She doesn't realize that reading subversive communist literature could get us all in trouble. I'm not sure what the repercussions might be, but this friend will have to call around tomorrow and take the book away. That's the problem. She's old enough to be left on her own all day, but I can't control what's going on when I'm not here.

Today I was a wreck at work! My new boss called me into his office to show me an overtime sheet for one of the other secretaries on the floor. We do get paid overtime, but we generally don't make a claim unless it's a big project and we're working very long hours. I gasped when I saw the claim. She put in six hours on Saturday, the same on Sunday, and three hours each evening. The matter was highlighted by the payroll department, who conducted an audit of overtime. Well, the claim is genuine because it's been signed by her boss, but I can't figure out why she should be working all these hours. My boss asked me to stay behind each evening and make a note of when she leaves this week. I wanted to shout, "No, I can't do it. I've got a family to look after!" but what's the use? This guy knows very little about me and cares even less. I just muttered that I couldn't do it tonight but would make some arrangements. Jack would never have made such a demand on me! I couldn't say no, but now I'll have a teenage daughter at home in the evenings, totally unsupervised. Even worse, Tamara will have to stay longer at the child minder's and will be bad-tempered and hungry. Any extra money I might earn from this imposition will end up in the pocket of that damned child minder! I suppose I'll have to call Stanley and hope he can stop by for a few evenings.

The only bright spot in the day was Su's driver's license, which arrived in the mail. She was so excited to tell me when I got home. She feels all grown-up now and wants to know when she can have her own car, like all her friends. Teenagers seem to think that money grows on trees. Yet another thing I'll have to talk to Stanley about. Maybe he can work something out. Perhaps he has a contact in the auto business who can come up with a plan.

Oh, I wish I could turn back the clock and still be working for Jack! Better still, I wish I was in Grace's shoes; all she seems to do is play golf or attend an art class or have lunch at some fancy restaurant. It must be wonderful to be so carefree and financially secure!

Grace 12

I'm so glad to get today over with—the dreaded MRI scan. I was a little bit reckless today. I should have arrived two hours early at the radiology center and then taken the tranquilizer so that I wasn't driving under the influence of drugs, but Edward phoned just as I was about to leave the house; he rarely calls and was in a chatty mood, and I didn't want to cut him off, so I let him ramble on; he didn't seem to notice that I was distracted and not saying very much. Before I knew it, time had slipped away, so I had to tell him I had a medical appointment. He quickly took notice and asked me all about the scan. He was so encouraging, telling me not to worry, that everything would be all right. I was running late and realized there wasn't enough time to sedate myself at the radiology center and wait for the effects. I should have arranged for someone to drive me there, but I didn't want to bother anyone, and I didn't want to tell anyone about the scan. To make sure I was relaxed for the scan, I took the tranquilizer just as I left the house. I had to make a decision: risk falling asleep at the wheel or suffering the noise and claustrophobia of the MRI scan. I took the risk...not like me at all. I'm normally very cautious. It takes thirty minutes to reach Arlington Boulevard, so I kept the radio on full blast and the air-conditioning blowing right into my face to keep me awake. I kept punching the steering wheel and yelling at all the other drivers on the road to keep my adrenalin going. Thankfully, avoiding any lane changes in the traffic, I made it without any mishap and even bagged a parking spot right at the front door. I sat in the car, waiting for the drug to take effect, but nothing seemed to happen.

Eventually, I was forced to make my way to the front desk, still feeling wide awake. I offered to let other patients go before me, but that didn't work. I had to take my appointment, on time, and meet the staff. The technician was very relaxed and tucked me into the MRI machine with blankets to keep me warm and gave me earmuffs to deaden the noise. I also brought my own earplugs, which I stuffed into place. I waited for the banging noises to start; somehow, the noises didn't bother me too much… loud bangs every time they take a picture; maybe the drug *had* taken effect.

An hour later, it was over and I was back in the waiting room. Feeling relieved to have the experience behind me, I bought myself a coffee and a sandwich from the café. I went back to the car with the intention of enjoying lunch on the go before driving back home. Two hours later, I woke up, never having drunk the coffee or eaten the sandwich. I fell fast asleep in the car, right there in the parking lot…for two hours. I dread to think what might have happened if I had started the journey home.

I'm okay with all of this; talking to Edward calmed my fears a little. I made him swear not to tell Jessica or Jack about the scan. If I have to deal with multiple sclerosis or Lyme's disease, I can do it; it's not the end of the world. I know it will affect all of my circumstances: my home life, my social life, our finances, our retirement plans, my relationship with Jack, but I'll just have to deal with all of it. I'll simply carry on as long as I can, doing as much as I can; the decline will probably be gradual rather than dramatic. Right now, I'm still feeling a little out of whack with that tranquilizer. I get the results of the scan tomorrow.

Kendra 12

I was late for work today because the traffic around Tyson's was so terrible! I just managed to grab a cup of coffee from the kitchen and slump into my chair with relief, when the human resources manager buzzed me to say the receptionist had called in sick. This means that all the senior secretaries have to take turns manning the reception desk. Well, what do you know, but I was allocated to spend the morning at the front desk because the others are putting the final touches to a conference that starts tomorrow. The company doesn't like junior staff at the reception desk; the preference is to have us executive assistants be the alternative first impression because we're normally dressed in business suits. So I had to waste my morning being polite to total strangers!

My boss is giving a presentation to the board tomorrow afternoon. I hadn't done his slides, and that reception desk never stopped; loads of visitors; signing for Fedex, DHL, and UPS deliveries; the switchboard winking all the time; and no lunch break.

Well, what do you know? The receptionist didn't turn up in the afternoon, and, somehow, I got stuck at the front desk for the whole day. I was expected to prepare all the slides for tomorrow's presentation while manning the reception desk at the same time. Seems like everyone else is more important than me! Jack would never have allowed this to happen! So that was more wasted time for me sitting there, answering the phones, while I had much better things to do.

The afternoon started off okay. All was quiet. A call came in from one of the engineers to speak to his boss, who wasn't around. The engineer didn't want to leave a voicemail but asked me to put a note on his boss's desk. I walked up the corridor, put the note on the desk, and went further along to take a look into the secretarial bays. Nobody around; they were all in the conference room, so no way for me to get a cup of coffee. The kitchen is right there, so I quickly nipped in to grab a cup of coffee and came back to the front desk. Standing there, waiting for me, was one of the presidents. I got such a lecture about leaving the desk unattended. He thundered at me that we're a government contractor, with security clearance, so nobody is allowed past reception unless accompanied by a member of staff. A stranger could have walked through and read all our confidential documents. I tried to explain my predicament, but he was shouting and making such a scene! Everybody in the company could hear me getting a dressing down. It was all very humiliating!

A few hours later, the human resources manager came to see me, stating that the situation was very serious. This president guy has lodged a formal complaint. Apparently, he's the compliance officer, and if there are any problems with security, he could be jailed. Well, I do understand the huge responsibility and all the repercussions, but for heaven's sake, I only went for a cup of coffee! Nobody entered the building in my absence. It won't happen again. I apologized, acknowledged that I made a mistake, and took full responsibility for my actions. Well, that's just not enough it seems! My little transgression has sparked off a huge investigation into potential security lapses. My name is at the front of the investigation. Who would have thought a cup of coffee could cause such havoc?

I won't get a wink of sleep tonight. I might lose my job over this situation. No job means no everything—no salary, no benefits, no nothing. If only Jack was still my boss; he would have defended me! I'm dreading going to work tomorrow.

Grace 13

I had a lovely escape from the confines of the house over the weekend. Miriam called on Friday to say she wanted to go on a shopping trip to Leesburg, so I was more than happy to tag along. I do love having Miriam in the neighborhood; I guess she's my closest friend, now, after all these years. I suppose I should have asked her to drive me to the radiology center for the MRI scan, but then I would have to tell her all about my health issues, and that's private. I don't want anyone to know about my health issues. Anyway, off we went, battling the construction traffic around Tyson's, arriving just in time for lunch at Lightfoot's on King Street. Miriam was looking for an antique lamp for her sitting room, so we toured the charming antique stores. She didn't find a lamp but bought a stash of antique crystal glasses.

A wonderful afternoon followed. I should have called the doctor's office for the results of the MRI scan, but Jack came home from his trip to England just as I arrived back from Leesburg, so I was more than happy for an excuse not to find out the results of the scan. I wasn't dressed for cooking a meal, so we decided to go to the Galleria and choose something light from the menu at the Lebanese Taverna. Strolling around the mall afterward, we gazed in the window of the Wentworth Gallery. A huge painting caught Jack's attention; he found the painting quite intriguing, very contemporary, vivid colors, lots of symbolism and touches of whimsy; he thought it would look fantastic in our family room. I didn't expect Jack to like the painting, but he was really enthusiastic. Maybe it was jetlag from his trip to England, but he liked several paintings in the gallery. So without intending to buy anything that evening, Jack arranged for the art consultant to bring the paintings to our home for consideration.

Driving past the Melkite Church on the way home, Jack wondered how much money the Middle East food festival raised last week; his bet was around eighty thousand dollars. He decided he wanted to attend the Sunday morning service so that he could check the result.

As Sunday morning dawned, I thought Jack's impulse for church attendance would be forgotten, but he was determined to check out his business instincts. As we arrived, I felt like an extra in a movie. There were lots of holy men parading around in embroidered vestments, lots of chanting by the congregation, lots of incense and jingling bells—the whole experience was a sensory overload. At last, the moment of truth arrived. The priest announced the takings from last week were almost ninety thousand dollars. So Jack won his bet!

As we were leaving, a young man approached and asked if we would like to join the congregation for coffee and doughnuts. I accepted the invitation, while Jack looked most uncomfortable. We were introduced to a young woman who told us of the life of sin she had rejected. It was curious for a perfect stranger to make a public confession to us. I could have stayed longer to hear more about her life, but Jack wanted to prepare for a trip to New York in the morning. I'm left feeling envious that these people have such a sense of community and a feeling of awe for the piety and devotion of the worshippers…these people seem to have a dimension in their life that doesn't exist in mine.

Reflecting on the events of the weekend, I just realized what my life is all about! It's all about Jack! He gets to know the result of a church fund raiser, but I don't get to know the result of the MRI scan!

Kendra 13

My work situation is very tense. I went to see the human resources manager this morning. I explained what happened on the day I left the reception desk unattended. I asked him if any action would be taken. He looked hesitant. I told him I was a single parent with three children and that I need to work. He simply said, "We'll leave it at that." I don't know if that means there will be no action or whether it means he was not prepared to discuss the matter further. I felt that pressing him would just make things worse. I can't influence the situation.

My boss has been fairly hostile since my little incident. This morning, he was more pleasant but asked if we could have lunch together. I thought he meant just a sandwich at the desk, but he asked me to make a reservation at L'Auberge in Great Falls. I felt very uneasy when I called the restaurant. I was almost crossing my fingers that the restaurant would be fully booked. Normally, I would be thrilled at going to such an upscale place, but I had the feeling this might be a farewell lunch—the civilized way of getting fired. I was anticipating I would hear all the positive noises about my technical skills, but maybe it was time for a change.

I was feeling fairly somber as I got out of the car. The weather matched my mood—high winds and grey skies. Leo was waiting inside, with a polite and charming smile on his face. The smiling assassin! I decided to make the most of the situation and ordered the most expensive things on the menu. I chose foie gras and venison, and ordered a pricey bottle of wine. Very bold, but I planned to be fired in style! The food was wonderful, and the wine loosened my tongue. We talked about the weather, automatic payments for utility bills, and the traffic problems on the Beltway. Then came dessert and coffee—always the point when the real discussion takes place, so I was holding my breath.

I was quite puzzled when Leo voiced a complaint about my attitude. I've been his secretary for only a few months. I hardly know him, really. I wanted to yell, "What about your attitude! You treat me like I'm not a real person!" He told me I lack empathy. He's under intense pressure at work, and he says when everything was more relaxed in the office, I was fine. Now with major business issues going on, he claims I don't realize he's stressed and I take it personally by being rude to him and that I'm distracted with personal issues. I was quite stunned! I was convinced he was going to fire me for the security breach at the reception desk. I asked him about that, but he just shook his head and said human resources were reviewing the matter. I told him I didn't think it was fair to keep me hanging on; either I should know that my job was in jeopardy or not. I need to know if I should be looking for another job. He told me I would need to change my approach. He also told me he liked me very much and he understood my personal circumstances were difficult. I muttered some insincere words about changing my attitude and promised to put work first rather than my personal life. He agreed to follow up with human resources to put me out of my misery regarding the security breach.

I suppose I feel relieved, and I suppose I got to know my new boss a bit better, but none of this does anything for my self-esteem. Everyone in the office knows about the security breach! I feel I'm the subject of water-cooler gossip. I wish I had accepted Jack's offer to join his new venture!

Grace 14

The doctor's office called at nine o'clock this morning. The doctor needs to speak to me about the MRI scan, the nurse said; I asked her to tell me the results, but she said she couldn't give me that information. The doctor wants to see me in person, she said, offering me an appointment in the afternoon. The drive to the doctor's office was very different from my last trip down Gallows Road. I drove as if I was in a trance. My whole body felt heavy, and my mind felt numb. I knew I had to prepare myself for the worst. I kept picturing myself in the doctor's office, listening to the results of the scan, but I couldn't hear anything. I could only see a picture; nobody's lips were moving—not mine, not the doctor's; he was holding a piece of paper in his hand; I was staring at him.

Hearing the news from the doctor's lips was like listening to a voice coming through a megaphone; his voice seemed so loud, his mouth seemed so big, and his teeth seemed so large; his words seemed to push through the walls of his office, as if they were too big for the building. My body felt as if it shrank to the floor and I had become a miniature person surrounded by a lake of water. I was powerless; I couldn't swim out of the lake. The only thing

I could hear was my heartbeat; it was pounding in my chest; my ears were on fire.

Making my way through the parking lot, I looked across at the spot where I had fallen asleep in the car, after the MRI scan, a few days ago. I felt as if I had left that person behind; that person had another life; the person who was walking out of the doctor's office was some kind of ghost, a person who didn't really exist, a person with no future.

Inside the car, I held my face in my hands. My face felt numb; my forehead hurt from the pressure inside my head. A few minutes later, I was wandering up the aisle of the pharmacy. I watched all the other members of the human race collecting their medication. What horrible symptoms does everyone else have? Somehow, I couldn't face the future. I turned away. Near the cash desk, my eye caught a soft toy, a huge brown bear... I lifted him down and held him to my chest...he was so comforting...so soft and warm...he seemed to hug me...as if he needed me... I needed a big brown bear to hug me... I took him home...he whispered his name to me...Bruno.

The clatter of the garage door opening was such a welcome sound. The drawbridge to my private world! I staggered into the house and threw myself on the bed. I bawled my eyes out. I cried and cried and cried. I howled like a child, left alone on a desert island, with no hope of rescue. I stretched out my hand for Bruno and clutched him to my chest... Bruno is my friend... Bruno will stay with me always. What about Jack? I need to tell him tonight; he'll know something is wrong. I can't hide this from him. Will Jack stay with me always?

Kendra 14

I got home today to find Su in bad form — worse than usual, I should say. She was so looking forward to receiving her driver's license and was thrilled, after hobbling out on her crutches (which she's done every day), to find her license in the mailbox. The only problem is the license describes her as a male with brown eyes. How this could happen is quite beyond me! Mind you, the day we were at the DMV, all the computers went down and we had to wait ten minutes for everything to power back up. I can only assume this was the cause of the mix-up. Anyway, now we have to go back down to the DMV and wait for who knows how long to get the description changed. The DMV won't take any action from telephone calls. We have to go back down in person so that Su can present herself and let them see that she really is a blue-eyed, blonde female. So more time will be wasted with another trek down to Gallows Road. Meanwhile, Su is itching to drive. She assures me she can because the problem is with her left leg only. I was hoping Stanley could come up with some form of transport for her, and he did figure something out—temporarily, that is. He's gotten a loaner car from a friend.

Su can use the car for a few weeks, and we'll see what happens next; he sort of hinted that he would buy her a new car.

We were in high spirits when the black Honda was delivered to the door at the weekend. It's far from new, but it sounds like it's working okay. So we decided to go for a whirl and do some girlie stuff, just the two of us. Stanley offered to look after the younger ones. Su and I headed off to the shops at Tyson's. I needed to pay my Macy's account, and Su decided she would drop me off at the door while she parked the car. I made my way straight into the home wares department on the third floor from the top level of the parking lot. After paying off the smallest amount possible on my card, I turned to make my way to the escalator. I needed to reach the shoe department on the first floor, where I had arranged to meet up with Su. Stuffing my wallet into my bag, I looked up and caught a glimpse of someone who looked like Jack. Sure enough, it was him. I watched him walk toward a woman who was admiring some Waterford crystal. They smiled at each other and walked away together. I assume the woman was Grace; she looks elegant—slim, dark hair, not like me, at all. No doubt, she was planning the tableware for her next fancy dinner party. I imagined myself as the hostess of a dinner party, with Jack at the other end of the table. I would be wearing a designer dress, everything would be elegant, everyone smiling, while their expensive cars were parked outside in the driveway of my beautiful home. I brought myself down to earth quickly as Su tugged on my sleeve to tell me she had an accident in the parking lot.

Grace 15

I feel so ashamed of myself...crying like a baby about the results of the scan. I just needed to get it all out of my system. My future has changed! I suppose I was grieving! I suppose I *am* grieving. I felt like my heart had been ripped out!

Now, I'm feeling quite serene...the knowledge that something different is happening to my body, but the rest of the world doesn't know...a secret. Unlike pregnancy, with the knowledge that a wonderful new creation was growing inside of me, I now have a foreign invader taking over my body.

Edward phoned yesterday to find out the results of the scan; he didn't say much. He was shocked, I suppose; he says he wants to come and see me so that we can talk things over together. I made him promise not to tell anyone—not Jessica, not Jack, not anyone...not yet.

After Edward phoned, I spent a long time thinking. It was strange looking out the window at all the signs of spring— daffodils and magnolia blossoms bringing hope for the future. What does my future hold? Perhaps no change, at first, until I have my first "episode," as the doctor called it. I don't know if I do have the strength to deal with all this.

I keep trying to find the right moment to tell Jack, but it hasn't happened yet. Last night when he came home, after I got the scan result, he did look at me strangely and asked if I was okay, but then his cell phone rang and he paced all over the house, talking business for almost an hour. It was quite late; he had been at the Redskins game against the Philadelphia Eagles at Fedex Field with some potential new clients. I didn't expect him home until the early hours of the morning, but he said that, by half time, the game looked like it was over, with the Eagles in the lead and the Redskins showing no hope of recovery, so they all decided to leave early. Jack looked tired and preoccupied, so I held back from saying anything. I need to find the right moment. We've not been getting along too well, recently. That's another reason why it's hard to bring up the subject. Most nights we've been bickering at each other, mostly about what to watch on television. I want to watch current affairs programs at night, but Jack says he's had enough of the business world and politics by the time he gets home; all he wants to do is chill out by watching anything that is a switch off from work. A few nights ago, he told me I was a control freak because I didn't want the television turned to the sports channels; he stomped upstairs and slept in the spare room without bothering to say good night and then left in the morning without saying good-bye. Maybe Jack will be in a better mood tonight; then I can broach the subject. It's not like I'll be telling him I've got six months to live, which would be easier than telling him I, probably, have multiple sclerosis. Effectively, I'll be telling him I could be a burden for the next twenty or thirty years... I don't want that... I don't want to be a burden to Jack or to my children.

Kendra 15

Somehow I got entangled with other people's families today! I volunteered to help at a birthday party for a neighbor's daughter. I don't know them very well, but Tamara was invited, so it seemed like a friendly gesture. Most of the kids were fine, apart from one boy who was very aggressive. He was constantly pushing and shoving the other little ones. He's quite a burly little boy, so he can muscle others out of the way quite easily. It wasn't long before the other kids were telling me he was threatening to kill them. Mostly, I don't bother with telltales, but this was quite disturbing! Next thing I knew, he took a crayon and pretended to stab himself in the stomach, yelling, "This is my life! Death! I kill myself." I discovered the boy behaves like this all the time but everyone puts his violent behavior down to watching TV. It seems that other mothers tolerate this kind of stuff since they live in fear of repercussions from the parents. My conscience wouldn't let me walk away from this situation, so I spoke to his father when he came to collect the boy. I thought the father would be defensive, but surprisingly, he thanked me for letting him know. This little boy is a danger, not only to himself but to everyone around him. He's only five years old! What will he be like ten years from now?

All I wanted when I got home was a cup of coffee, but what do I find but Su comforting a school friend. This teenager comes from a nice home, but the mother is a cruel bully who threw her down the stairs during a drunken rage. The girl had an ugly bruise on her face and looked so desperate that I took pity on her. I've met her before. She's always very quiet and polite, but you can see the fear in her eyes. I got her helping Su to make dinner for all of us. Not difficult. Simply boiling pasta and throwing a jar of sauce over some leftovers. It was a way of deflecting her emotions and making her feel safe and welcome. As we sat around the table, I gazed at this girl, just imagining how she might end up. She needs a safe haven, and she's not getting it at home. Who knows what might happen to her if she runs away from home? While we cleared the table, I asked if she wanted to stay overnight. She closed her eyes and nodded. "Call your mom," I told her. "Tell her where you are." I want the mother to know I can be a witness to the girl's injuries, if necessary. At bedtime, I told this vulnerable girl she can stay overnight anytime she wants. Under my roof, she'll have my protection whenever she needs it.

Maybe I should mind my own business! I have enough problems of my own, but I can't stand aside when children are at risk.

Grace 16

I checked my calendar this morning and realized I should be at a fundraising lunch in the Ritz Carlton at Tyson's Corner. The last thing I felt like doing was getting dressed up and sitting around making small talk, but I decided to attend. Once coffee was served, everyone settled down to listen to the speaker. The charity operates alongside the police to provide comfort to women and children who've been attacked or abused. The women are provided with comfortable clothing while their belongings are DNA tested by the police. The children are provided with handmade comfort pillows, heart shaped with little pockets full of goodies such as tiny dolls or candy. Hearing all the awful stories of abuse touched everyone's heart... I expect the donations were generous.

I did have trouble keeping my emotions in check at this luncheon. I thought back to my involvement with the Farthing Foundation. All those years of involvement wasted; in some ways, I regret pulling out. It was a huge mistake agreeing to become the treasurer. I felt as if I was treated like hired help, driving all over the place to hand-deliver checks to various people at a moment's notice. I do acknowledge that I let my irritation show whenever these situations arose; perhaps I should just have taken it all in my stride. I don't remember ever complaining, but I do remember, at the end of the year, making it known that it's not an easy job and the next incumbent should expect to spend a lot more time on the position than expected. Well, I thought I was being helpful by giving advice for the next person, but it came across as plain speaking and caused quite a stir. I think back to that time and how upsetting the whole situation became—a lot of board members supporting me and threatening to resign if future treasurers were expected to make this kind of commitment; other members resenting my view of things. I remember how uncomfortable I felt. It was such a relief to pull out at the end of the year, but I really miss everyone… I just love them all and have a great feeling of loss at not being involved. Everything and everyone has moved on since then. I can't go back. Maybe I should just have kept quiet and not given my honest views. Maybe I should have just swallowed the discomfort and stayed with the group.

Well, it's too late. It's all in the past. However, if there's something I would change in life, it would be taking on that particular responsibility… I'm hopeless with money… I was so happy in the group before then… I do miss everyone. They're a wonderful bunch of people… I miss seeing all those people whose company I really enjoyed… Jack misses them too. It's all my fault. I can't recover from the past. I do have regrets. I know I just have to move on. How to move on is another matter… I've just been pushing it to the back of my mind. My life has become diminished. My energy level is low. I'm feeling exhausted from that lunch today.

Kendra 16

Well, the repairmen all let me down on Saturday morning! The appliance guy fitted a new motor to the ice dispenser, but the new motor turned out to be faulty; that means we have to wait another few weeks for him to get hold of a replacement motor and we have to be disturbed, again, to let him into the apartment. The guy who was due to fix the doorbell didn't turn up. The broken shade from the window was taken away by the installer; it needs to go back to the manufacturer, so now, instead of a faulty shade on the window, we have nothing at all. I do worry constantly about the scary man who is making an insurance claim against Su for her bump in the parking lot. He could be staring in the windows at night!

In the meantime, I have to do everything I can to keep my job but, at the same time, look for another position. On Saturday afternoon, I registered with a couple of recruitment agencies. The first one was terrible; an untidy young woman with a disinterested attitude asked me to fill in forms. I told her I wasn't going to fill in any forms until I had established whether I wanted to use her services. I requested to be interviewed in a more private arrangement where I asked for details of vacancies for executive assistants, but was told this information was available to me only after filling in all their forms and taking a series of tests. I wasted no time in getting out of their scruffy office!

My next approach was an agency with an international reputation who gave a much better account of themselves. I was interviewed in a private office and took a bunch of tests, and afterward, I was introduced to all the staff. Everyone was dressed in dark business suits and exuded energy. So, I left my future in the hands of Dominion Personnel. With a lighter heart, I exited the parking lot, only to be asked to hand over ten dollars at the barrier! I've got to make more money somehow!

My next approach has been to post my resume on some websites. Now, all my personal information is dangling in cyberspace! Anybody can see my home address, e-mail address, phone number, as well as my current and previous employers. I know I don't have a choice, but it's terrifying. I started thinking about Jack. I really should have moved with him to the new venture. I swallowed my pride and called his cell phone. He seemed pleased to hear from me. I didn't want to ask for a job outright, so I asked him all about Spelectra. He was full of enthusiasm, saying the company has a great future. At last, he asked how things were going for me. I told him about the security breach and how I don't like working for Leo. I didn't actually say, "I miss you, Jack." I was hoping he could read between the lines.

So with not much hope in the business scene, I decided to approach Fairfax County to register as a substitute teacher. The first thing you have to do is take a web-based interview. The website tells you that good teachers score well on this test, so it's used instead of face-to-face interviews. The interview seemed to assess attitudes and values. I'm quite sure I won't be accepted. One question, which I think will fail me, asked if I had ever broken the rules, to which I answered, "Not often." I'm sure that's not what they want. They want teachers who will unwaveringly stick to the rules. Well, that just isn't me. My view is that you need to be able to use your judgment in particular situations.

So lots of effort with no results! I wish I had a magic wand to change my circumstances!

Grace 17

I keep trying to push everything to the back of my mind, but it's hard. I keep trying to find the right moment to tell Jack, but it hasn't happened yet. The longer I leave it, the harder it becomes. I think he'll be angry that I've kept it from him, but it's been a busy weekend, so there wasn't the right opportunity.

Jack invited people from New York to spend the weekend with us. I would have been okay with that normally, but I couldn't muster the enthusiasm for running round, getting everything ready, and then smiling all the time at his business associates. The arrangements were to take them to the Stratford Culinary School for dinner on Friday night. I didn't realize the culinary school is part of Stratford University in Falls Church. The students did a fine job; dinner was served buffet style, and the quantities were gargantuan. As we were leaving, the students were smiling broadly as they carted away the leftovers, presumably to share with their friends. I hope they had a great evening.

Saturday dawned—a crisp, beautiful day. Bright blue skies were a stunning backdrop for the amazing colors adorning our tall and stately Virginia trees. Good weather for the drive to Mount Vernon. We spent the initial part of the day touring the education center, the museum, and the orientation center. I couldn't take all the walking around; my feet were tingling, and I had the oddest feeling of hot spots on my legs. The only respite was having lunch at Mount Vernon Inn. Just to sit down was a relief. Our guests decided to try the signature dish of chestnut-and-peanut soup as well as the bread pudding. We made our way toward the mansion, only to discover the wait time was thirty minutes, and there was a stiff breeze blowing. I excused myself by saying I was feeling very cold. I left Jack, with his shivering guests, darting in and out of all the outbuildings. No wonder George Washington was a reluctant president; he was dragged out of retirement from this wonderful plantation on the banks of the Potomac.

When we got home at the end of the day, there was a phone message from Edward. I forgot he said he might be dropping by this afternoon; we just missed him by half an hour. Jack was annoyed with me; he was also annoyed that I had gone back to sit in the car while his guests were still touring the plantation. I reminded him that I was feeling very cold, but he just said I should have worn something warmer and made a better job of looking after his guests.

The doctor wants me to have an electro-physiological test as a further method of confirming the diagnosis. Since my symptoms are mild, he suggested I just get on with my life in the meantime. Right now, I'm feeling tired all the time with a broken sleep pattern. My hands and feet are tingly, but not all of the time; it's much worse after I've been walking. I'll phone Edward in the morning; it will be good to get his advice on how to break the news to Jack.

Kendra 17

On Sunday, I took the kids to the Claude Moore Colonial Farm on Georgetown Pike. It was a glorious day, and the farm was the perfect place for an outing. The entrance fee didn't break the bank, which is a great relief since I have to watch the pennies now. I really don't know what my finances are going to be like in the foreseeable future!

We were greeted by a gaggle of geese announcing our arrival by squawking loudly. Geese make great security guards! We trailed past the tobacco plantation to arrive outside the home of the farmer and his family, who were dining outdoors, dressed in typical eighteenth-century costume, with mud clinging to their bare feet, just like in colonial times. Their Sunday lunch consisted of bean stew and cornbread, which they cooked on an open fire inside their wooden house. The farmer invited us to look inside their home. The shelter is functional, about the size of a double garage. The roof has a steep pitch, with mattresses in the loft where the whole family sleep together. Outside, a wonderful rooster, with colorful feathers, was pecking at food remnants from a pan that had been used to cook the meal. Nearby a cow watched as one of the boys herded up wild turkeys and hogs into pens, ready for slaughter. The children asked lots of questions at the farm but were very quiet on the way home. I think the visit shocked them into realizing how lucky they are.

I felt lonely today! I would have felt a whole lot better if the children had a father figure in their life. Stanley is so unreliable; he did say he was coming with us today, but typical Stanley, he called at the last minute to say he couldn't make it. I didn't even ask him for a reason. I just told the kids he couldn't join us today; they looked disappointed because they do enjoy his company. That's just the thing. Stanley is so easy to be around—when it suits him to be here. But he always lets you down. If only I had a man like Jack! I've never known Jack to be unreliable!

Grace 18

The New York visitors took care of themselves today—a miserable, wet Sunday after the beautiful weather we've been enjoying. They took themselves off to the Basilica downtown; apparently, it holds the largest display of contemporary religious art in the world. We wanted to give this a body swerve. We're not religious people. Religion is the opium of the people, they say. I could do with some opium at the moment.

We arranged to meet our visitors for dinner in the evening, at Tuscora Mill in Leesburg. I thought there would be an opportunity to tell Jack before we went…a quiet Sunday afternoon at home. Next thing I know, Jack tells me he's going to the golf club for some practice and perhaps play nine holes if the weather improves. After he left, I was really angry. Doesn't he realize there's something wrong with me! All he seems to think and talk about is Spelectra or golf. He's on the phone all the time at home. Business is booming, he tells me. The technology is going global, and he'll get a federal loan guarantee to expand internationally. After we got home from dinner last night, I told him I was tired and asked him to pack his own case prior to bedtime. Usually, he waits until the last minute, expects me to pack his case, and then stomps around, getting all task orientated when I'm feeling sleepy and just want to drop my head on the pillow.

Once his packing was all done, I said, "Jack, we need to talk," but he hardly looked up. His response was, "Yes, what are we going to do for Thanksgiving?" I just answered, quietly, that we would talk when he got back from Los Angeles. Then my temper flared, and I shouted, "In fact, why don't I send you an e-mail?"

I'm really downhearted now. Jack won't be able to cope with his business if I'm going downhill. What will our lives be like? I'll be stuck at home, getting steadily worse. Can I inflict that on Jack? He's so into this new venture; it could make a fortune for him—not just for him but the kids, too. The new venture means a lot of traveling for him; I did wonder if it was the right thing for him to do at his point in his life. There's no point in me reminding him that he had a heart attack last year; he just shrugged that off, lost some weight, keeps his cholesterol under control, and carries on, regardless. There's no doubt my declining health will mess things up, for everyone. These last few days of coping with visitors has tired me out. I'm feeling stressed, too. I should have been able to take all that in my stride, quite easily. A slower pace of life is in store for me. I just can't stand the thought of losing my independence.

Kendra 18

I took the kids to see mother this evening. Really, it was late and they should have been in bed, but they hadn't seen Grandma for ages; she's quite a remarkable woman; eighty years old with lots of friends. I could never have imagined her living the way she does—playing poker and mahjong and traveling around the country, ever since Dad passed. We've not seen her for two whole months because she's spent a month in New York and a month in Atlanta.

Grandma was in fine form. I can't believe it; she has a date tomorrow night. At her age! She's joined several singles societies; she likes to be in male company. Playing poker is, of course, another way of meeting the opposite sex! Anyway, there she was, looking just terrific. She's always full of fun. Everyone falls in love with her; they just have to realize she has a will of iron. Her date tomorrow night is with a man she met while standing in line at the bank. He's much younger than her (seventy-one years old) but remains on the board of a chain of hotels. I liked the steady boyfriend she had for a couple of years, but he wanted to stay home all the time. She says she can stay home by herself; she doesn't need company for that. Now she only wants to date men who are still working! I'm not sure what planet my mother inhabits. What I wouldn't give to meet a man who has a chain of hotels! Apparently, her date is at the Panache Restaurant in Tyson's Corner. She hasn't been there before and loves to go to new places. I'm looking forward to the critique of the restaurant, not to mention the lowdown on her date! We didn't stay too long since the kids got hungry, and Grandma doesn't cook. I thought she would hate that condo in Reston, but she's settled in really well and made lots of new friends.

I didn't mention any of my problems to Mother; not the work situation, or the scary man who had the accident with Su, or the maintenance problems in the apartment, or the lack of support from Stanley. My mother deserves to have fun and enjoy seeing her grandchildren. She doesn't need to be burdened with any of my worries.

I was amazed to learn I got through the online interview for substitute teaching. I now have to deal with all the bureaucracy. I keep hoping Jack might call me, but I don't expect that's going to happen. Jack has no reason to get in touch with me. I suppose Jack has forgotten all about me. I think I'll give him a call.

Grace 19

I'm feeling so tired! Edward came to see me this afternoon. I tried to prepare what I was going to say to him. I needed to tell him all the symptoms of multiple sclerosis and the prognosis. I wanted to talk over all the practicalities. Edward is a thoughtful boy; he's always been like that, ever since he was little. Funny how kids enter the world with their own personality. Now he's going to be my confidante—that's nothing new, really.

Edward has always been my first thought whenever I'm anxious about something. When I told him, he gave me a long hug. Then he asked, "How long have you got, Mom?" I suppose he could see I was in bad shape emotionally and assumed the worst. Somehow, his soulful expression brought on the tears, but I pulled myself together quickly. I explained the cause of the disease and the symptoms and what I might expect in the future. He just kept nodding, saying very little. I told him Jack didn't know yet; I hadn't found the right time to tell him. Edward was very alarmed and said, "You need to do that soon, Mom." Then things felt a bit awkward. I changed the conversation by asking what was going on in his life. He told me there were lots of parties going on but I wouldn't want to know about them. I smiled and asked if there was anyone special in his life. He replied by saying, "Haven't you guessed by now?" I instantly knew what he meant but wasn't sure how to respond. So I replied by saying, "Whatever it is, son, you better just come right out with it." After a pause, he stated, "I prefer guys."

Deep down, I've known all along. Ever since he was a young boy, Edward didn't seem to fit in anywhere. The day I found Jessica's underwear and one of her dresses hidden in the bottom drawer of his armoire, I knew things weren't right. I told myself it was just a boy's prank because Jessica had been looking for that dress for weeks; it was one of those signals that always burrowed into my brain, but I didn't want to face the possibility. "Don't tell Dad," he insisted. "I've been meaning to tell him for ages. I'll do it, eventually." I sighed and stared at the floor. "So, now we both have secrets from Dad."

I've been treating Edward as a companion for too long; it's not right. I'm still doing it now, confiding in him when I should be confiding in Jack. I wish he hadn't told me…not now anyway.

Kendra 19

I can't concentrate on anything today! I have a dermatologist appointment this evening to deal with some basil cells that have popped up. I have to be so vigilant and catch these before they develop into the next level of skin cancer. Also, I'm waiting for the guy to reinstall the faulty shade on the bedroom window. He should have been here at eight o'clock this morning, but he's late. I phoned his office, and they assure me he's on his way. It will be such a relief to have privacy at that window. It's been really spooky thinking the scary guy from Su's car accident might be looking in here at night. So now I'll be late for work!

Thanksgiving is tomorrow. I've done all the grocery shopping. I've gotten a lovely fresh turkey and a huge pumpkin pie. Grandma is bringing her special stuffing that the kids actually hate, but they pretend like they love it. I'll certainly be giving thanks tomorrow since I get to keep my job. What a relief! The human resources manager called me into his office yesterday to discuss the matter. My legs were shaking, and my guts turned to jelly. However, he was relaxed and smiling, so my hopes were high. A note about my misdemeanor will be kept on file for a year and then destroyed.

Actually, I find that offensive. I would almost rather be fired than have a cloud hanging over me. I'm not sure what the law states in these circumstances, but I don't have the time or energy to make enquiries. I suppose I'm expected to bring up the subject again a year from now and request that the note on my file is removed. All because I left the reception desk for a few minutes! I think I'll still look for another job.

I called Jack last night. This time I was more direct. "Hi, Jack. Just wanted to keep in touch. I'm on the lookout for another job," was my opening line. He asked what was making me want to move. I just said I didn't like working for Leo; he didn't ask for more information. I asked him all about Spelectra and showed a great interest in all the details; he's very enthusiastic about the whole venture. I finished the call by saying, "Well, if you hear of any positions that might suit me, do pass my name along."

The next turkey dinner we'll be eating will be on Christmas Day. Now the difficulties start. Where will we spend the day? Nothing will be ideal. The perfect scenario is for my kids to be with their mother and father, along with grandparents and other family members. Well, it's not gonna be like that. If only the kids had a decent father—someone like Jack. I just wonder how many people in this vast land will be spending Christmas Day in circumstances that are not ideal. It's the saddest day of the year for so many people. Maybe we could help the Salvation Army. I passed a guy outside the grocery store yesterday ringing his bell for the Salvation Army. I popped a few dollars into his bucket. He responded with, "Have a happy Christmas." I replied, "You too." He answered, "I'll try." He was quite a young man, but he looked so sad. We really should try to do something for strangers on Christmas Day.

Grace 20

Thanksgiving Day was very successful. Our guests arrived, bearing gifts in great holiday mood; we were showered with flowers, champagne, wine, and chocolates. I decided to use my deep fryer for the turkey; I bought it three years ago but never used it. Today was the ideal opportunity, and the contraption kept Jack amused outside, tinkering with the device. My eighteen-pound turkey dipped into four gallons of hot oil was ready in one hour. I made pumpkin soup from scratch, along with my special corn bread, although I did buy the pecan pie. What a joy to have the energy to do all these things. It really was fun to have the house full of visitors. Everyone seemed to have a good time.

Jessica and Edward made their way to us without much trouble in traffic. Edward was very quiet all day. He felt uncomfortable, I know. I think he was hoping we would both have shared our secrets by now, but there hasn't been the right opportunity. Of course, having guests prevented any discussion on the subject today, which was a great relief for me. Also, if everyone knew about my MS, they would pity me... I'm not ready for that. Jack is blissfully unaware of the situation. I didn't want to spoil

Thanksgiving by giving him my news. It's ironic that he enquired when I was having my annual physical. I told him I wasn't going to bother just yet.

I actually feel quite good at the moment. I've been trying a change of diet and taking some herbal remedies; it does seem to help. My only thoughts now are for Jack, Jessica, and Edward. If only my thoughts could turn into wishes granted. I wish Jack didn't have to travel so much. I wish Jessica could find a nice young man and settle down. I wish Edward would feel able to tell Jack and Jessica about his choice of lifestyle. He was fairly withdrawn over Thanksgiving; he can be quiet and reserved but usually makes an effort when we have guests; however, he was quite remote and barely spoke to anyone over dinner. He excused himself soon after, saying he had personal phone calls to make, which was really rather rude.

Somehow I have no wishes for myself. The wishes for my family can be granted but not mine. I can't wish for multiple sclerosis to disappear; that's not going to happen... I just have to accept it, but the terror and the tears are never far away. The doctor told me I should expect to have an "episode," which is a period of at least one day when I'm not able to function normally, such as inability to walk or acute fatigue that prevents routine daily activity. I think I've had some kind of episodes in the past. There have been days when I was fit for nothing—just no energy. I've never had trouble walking, but my balance is often very poor. I always have to be careful when getting up from a table or out of the car. It's difficult to get to sleep, and I keep waking up dreaming of Jessica. I keep seeing her in a muddy pond, drowning... I throw her a stick, but she never catches it.

Kendra 20

Thanksgiving was a very pleasant day! Grandma arrived at noon wearing a multi-colored cardigan and clutching her special stuffing. I'm so budget-conscious right now, so I made some soup yesterday along with some cornbread. The soup turned out fine; stock cubes combined with leftover vegetables I stored in the freezer made a great soup when pureed in the blender. So that was lunch. Dinner worked out really well, apart from the turkey; I miscalculated the cooking time, and it was quite dried out. I skipped the appetizer and went full throttle to get all the vegetables and trimmings ready at the same time. Thankfully, it all worked out!

So then the clean-up began. While the kids cleared the dishes, I stripped the carcass of the turkey. We have enough left over in the freezer now to provide us with several meals. I used the carcass, along with the neck and giblets, to make a stock for another batch of soup. I peeled some carrots, added that to the stock, and then threw in all the leftover vegetables. After seasoning, it all tasted great, so I went straight into blending. Unfortunately, I overfilled the blender and was assailed with scalding soup on my face and neck. Luckily, it missed my eyes. I spent the next fifteen minutes with an ice pack on the injured areas.

Meanwhile, Grandma took over the clearing up. All went well but suddenly became very quiet. I looked across to see the children with shocked looks on their faces. Grandma's cardigan was on fire. The candle from the centerpiece on the table had set her alight. Not a word was spoken as she smothered the flames with a napkin. Thankfully, she was wearing a cotton shirt underneath, so her skin wasn't burned. I changed places with Grandma, who sank into the sofa, a forlorn expression on her face and her ruined cardigan on her lap.

I finally sank into the sofa beside Grandma to try and relax. I browsed through the *Viva Tysons* magazine. My eye was caught by the Black Friday advertisement. Stores are doing big specials from midnight until five o'clock. Every hour, there are free giveaways, such as tote bags, umbrellas, ice scrapers, and cups of coffee. Shoppers who arrive in pajamas have VIP access to the food court for breakfast items. Live entertainment goes on all day. I would just love to go to the mall tomorrow. It would be such fun, and we wouldn't need to spend any money, although I guess I'll have to buy a new cardigan for Grandma.

I don't know where Stanley spent Thanksgiving. There was no reason why he couldn't spend the day with us. He hasn't been in touch with me or the children. Probably he went with some buddies on a trip somewhere. He really is irresponsible! The kids need a better father figure in their life!

Grace 21

I'm feeling quite buoyant for some reason. I don't feel tired anymore. I really feel optimistic. Spelectra is doing well, and Jack is full of enthusiasm. One more thing making me feel good is that I joined a health club. Apparently, exercise is advisable for keeping MS symptoms at bay, so I signed up last week. I'm really looking forward to the sessions with my personal trainer. I need to work on my balance; that could be a big problem in the future, so trying to get good muscle tone now seems like a good idea.

Jack still doesn't know anything. I need to tell him soon. There just is never the right time. We went to Starbucks for coffee, at the Galleria, on Saturday morning. I thought once Jack was relaxed I could tell him, but he didn't want to linger over coffee. He noticed that I stopped to admire a handbag in the window of the Chanel store; he offered to buy it for me, but I wouldn't hear of it, so we passed on. Returning to the car, I stopped at the window again, for just one last look at that adorable handbag. Jack, literally, dragged me into the store and made the purchase; it was most amusing. I was protesting all the while and tried to resist, but he held my arm tight and pulled me into the store with my feet trailing behind me. I don't suppose many stores see that kind of behavior. Anyway, I'm absolutely thrilled with the thing; it sits on a chair in the bedroom, and I admire it every day. Jack gets such pleasure from being the bearer of gifts!

Yesterday, Jack mentioned that Kendra's birthday is later this month; in the past, I always bought a gift for Jack to give to her; he asked me to do the same again this year. "But she doesn't work for you anymore," I protested. "Oh, just go and buy something, and mail it to her," he instructed. I have to admit I sulked a bit. I can't understand why he wants to keep that relationship going. Surely, mailing birthday gifts to her has to stop now that she's no longer his secretary. I'm trying not to feel angry and jealous, but I'll have to do what he asks. If I don't do it, there will be a scene. I've never even met Kendra! I did feel sorry for her when she was moving house, and we paid for her moving costs; that seemed like helping someone in need since she seemed to be in a financial mess, but now that Kendra is out of his life, I can't imagine why Jack would even think about her birthday. I'm the one who always thinks about birthdays, not Jack. He never thinks ahead about birthday gifts for Edward or Jessica. He never thinks ahead about birthday gifts for me!

Kendra 21

Today was the orientation for substitute teaching! I took a day's vacation from work to get registered. One foot wrong and the whole thing is out the window. I had all my documentation together, but I just noticed that the final document, my chest X-ray result, had not been signed. I had to race into the doctor's office this morning to get a signature. So, armed to the teeth, I drove down Gallows Road toward Fairfax County Public Schools administration office. I was most anxious to be on time. "Latecomers will not be processed," the confirmation letter stated. So, upon arrival, hordes of people were shepherded into the reception area, given tons of forms to fill in, and then moved along to a conference room where all our documents were checked. From there, we were directed to the fingerprint check area and then back to the conference room for orientation. We were called out in groups. It felt like boarding a budget airline or being drafted into the army. We were called in groups of numbers and had to line up to deal with the administrators.

I was overwhelmed with information on how to check in for work by phone and through the Internet. The whole thing is automated. I was very alarmed to find out that I could get a call as early as five o'clock in the morning to be placed on an assignment that day. It's also scary that I just checked boxes on what I thought I was able to teach and then I would arrive on the job alone, without any training, having to follow a lesson plan. Anyway, I won't get assignments until I do the final registration online.

This economy is hitting the education sector hard. There are five thousand substitute teachers in Fairfax County, with an average of nine hundred assignments each day. In the past, there would have been three times as many assignments daily, but with budget cuts, all kinds of other ways are found to fill the slots. We were given information on sexual harassment and walked through a bunch more forms. Some unfortunate people were turned away because their documentation did not meet requirements. We learned that we have to work ten days in a six-month period; otherwise, we become deregistered and have to go through the entire process all over again. We also learned that once we receive a call and accept an assignment, we have forty-five minutes to arrive at the school. Also, we can be terminated for being late, not having control of the class, and a bunch of other innocent misdemeanors. I came away with a headache. Do I really want to do this? I wonder if I had known, up front, that this was not going to be such an easy ride, would I have gone to all the effort of registering? It's taken months to get all the required documents together, not to mention the expense of driving all over the place. I'll have to be very careful of my personality trait of being too tenacious. I never know when to let go. Maybe I should let go of this teaching idea. It seems too regimented and too fraught with potential pitfalls. I'll have to see how it works out. Apparently, we should expect something in the mail within a week that will give us a special identity number that allows us to check in for assignments. Oh well! Let's see what happens. I just keep hoping Jack's new company might need me!

Grace 22

Sunday dawned with beautiful sunshine interspersed with a few clouds. Rising early, I was thrilled to see birds flitting around the trees. Normally, the foliage is so dense that we can hear the birds around us but rarely see them. Now there's barely a leaf on the trees. I stopped to admire a red cardinal that stayed motionless while keeping an eye on several energetic bluebirds.

My musings were, surprisingly, disturbed by Jack presenting me with a banana smoothie for breakfast; he never makes breakfast, so that was a nice surprise.

Last night, I did the laundry in the evening...something I never do. I always do the laundry while Jack is not around during the day. This week, I've been too tired to do any household chores. Anyway, Jack asked me to close the door of the laundry room since the noise was distracting him from watching television. I snapped back that the laundry room door was already closed, that he better get used to the noise, and that it's time he started learning how to do the laundry. We spent the evening apart. As Jack was getting ready for bed, I went into the bedroom holding my cell phone in my hand. I had to confess that I, accidentally, left the phone in the pocket of a pair of pants that had been in the washer. The noise we had been listening to in the evening must have been my phone thumping around inside the dryer in the laundry room. Jack shrugged and smiled.

Getting into bed, we snuggled up close. I was very quiet and motionless. Jack gently asked me what was wrong. With tears flowing, I told him I had been wanting to tell him for a long time, but there was never the right opportunity. He sat up in bed, listening intently. "Jack, I've had some tests at the doctor's. I've been diagnosed with multiple sclerosis." How often I had rehearsed those words. Now, I actually said them. It made the whole situation more real to me. Now it really is a problem. Before, it was just like something in the future that would need to be dealt with. Now, it's out in the open, and I'll have to focus on the practicalities. It seemed as if my self-esteem drained away as I gave Jack the news.

"How long have you known this?" was Jack's first question; he looked grim when he realized I had been keeping this from him for some time. He wanted to know all about the condition. "We'll just have to get the best doctors," was his view. It was difficult explaining to him that there's no cure for the condition. Yes, I can take medication to relieve the symptoms, but it's a degenerative disease.

"I don't want this to affect your life, Jack," I pleaded "It will affect my life, but there's no reason why you need to make any changes." He hugged me close but looked distracted. I know he was trying to work out all the possible scenarios. "You'll have whatever you need," he assured me. But I need him! I need to have company at home! Being left alone, all the time, was all right when I was fit and well and able to go out and do things, but I'm going to be more and more housebound as time goes on. Above all, I'm going to be lonely!

Kendra 22

Well, I didn't get a special identity number in the mail from Fairfax County! What I got instead was a phone call telling me my fingerprints were not processed. I would have to go back to the office to be processed again. At least it was a swift transaction. The assistant told me the fingerprints go through the FBI; he said the previous assistant hadn't done a good job. This time, a special pad was used to make my fingerprints more clear, and he told me not to press hard on the glass, so I thought that was the end of the matter. Not so! Another phone call a few days later. My fingerprints are still not accepted by the FBI. Back again to go through the process for a third time! A more experienced assistant told me that frequent hand washers often have this problem. Cleanliness renders your fingerprints indistinct. I waited for the next phone call. Thankfully, it never came! Another failure would have required a visit to the police station.

So a huge sigh of relief this morning when my special identification number came in the mail just as I was leaving for the office. I can now, officially, be an employee of Fairfax County Public Schools. I'm free to accept assignments once I complete the final registration online. It felt good to know there was another way of earning money if things go wrong at the office.

Becoming a registered substitute teacher gave me quite a feeling of achievement! It's been a time-consuming and frustrating experience. All sorts of thoughts were running through my head. I really don't need to take this course of action. My job should be safe. However, I have a distinct feeling of unease about remaining with the company. I feel my reputation has gone downhill. This morning, Leo called me into the office. I just knew he was going to give me a telling off. I felt like I was going to cry. I'm so ashamed of the mistakes I made. I know I'm not concentrating on my work. So when he closed the door of his office and asked me take a seat, I just couldn't bear the embarrassment and shame of being given a dressing down. Before I knew what was happening, I quit! I just couldn't, somehow, let him get the words out ahead of me. So I told him I was going to work as a substitute teacher. I found myself telling him I needed a career change, that this would be a step in the right direction, that I intended to get qualified and become certified. Leo seemed quite surprised. Not as surprised as me! I never intended to resign at this point. It just seemed the right thing to do on the spur of the moment. So, now I have a whole new life ahead of me. Actually, it all seems really crazy. I won't get any benefits. I don't know what came over me. I think I allowed pride to get in the way of prudence!

Grace 23

I told Miriam about the multiple sclerosis.
It was good to be able to unburden myself to an old friend.
Miriam was fantastic; she gave me a big hug and said, "You know
I'm here for you." Somehow, that's what I needed to hear from
Jack. I told her all about the disease and the prognosis and how
I should be taking more exercise to keep the symptoms at bay.
Next day, Miriam called to ask if I would be interested in joining
a hiking group. She wants to get a whole bunch of ladies together
to hike every day so there will always be someone doing the
activity with me. I was overwhelmed by Miriam's thoughtfulness,
and I reluctantly agreed. Hiking is not really my thing, but I do
need the exercise. Oddly enough, I don't feel embarrassed at
other people knowing about my condition now; it's a relief, really.
Whenever, I'm feeling exhausted and not good company, people
will make allowances. Anyway, we meet in Great Falls Park every
morning. If it's raining, we give it a miss. I really didn't think I
could cope with it all but was quite amazed that I managed to
keep pace with everyone. The only shock to the system was on
the trail called *Heartbreak*. It was okay going down, but coming
back up, I had to scamper up the hill to keep pace with everyone

else. At the top of the hill, I collapsed onto a log to catch my breath and was shocked to hear my heart hammering harder than I've ever heard it before. I can't believe I'm falling out of bed each morning to do this kind of thing. I can't believe how much I'm enjoying the experience. Walking in the wilderness is taking me back to my childhood... I suppose my childhood was idyllic... I didn't think so at the time, of course; children never do realize just how lucky they are. We could roam free as children in Virginia way back then. I remember those happy times with my older sisters... I still grieve for them every day, even now. If they were still alive, I would be talking with them on the phone, sharing my problems. Miriam is like a sister to me now. Our house on Morrissette Drive backed onto Lake Accotink, when we were children. We spent lots of time rowing a little boat together. We were never allowed to swim in the lake. Mother was always terrified of infections, but we used to do lots of hiking together, picking wildflowers, and skimming stones on the lake. I loved that little boat...such a beat-up, old thing, but I guess it made us strong, straining on those oars. Funny how much we quarreled about whose turn it was to row.

Thinking back to that lake brings back that dream I've been having about Jessica, drowning in the middle of a pond of muddy water and stretching her hands out to me, but I can't raise my hands to help her... I've had the dream several times.

Kendra 23

Stanley was furious when I told him I quit my job! I just lost it with him. I told him I have enough responsibility and now it's his turn. He'll just have to work harder to provide for his family. Even though we're not under the same roof, we're still his responsibility! Actually, I think he's been smoking again. He didn't smell too good. Somehow, that aroma of stale cigarette smoke made me feel superior to him. I don't know what he does with his life. I wonder if he has a woman somewhere. I don't care what he does, so long as the children are safe.

Everyone is in shock that I quit! I think they're quite envious that I've done something unpredictable! I leave the company at the end of the week. This evening, I looked online to see what teaching assignments might be available. I'm all set up on Smart Find Express, the website for substitute teachers to find work at local schools. I kept trying the website all evening but continually got the same message that nothing is available. I must admit that concerns me. I really thought there would be masses of work. I hope the downturn in the economy doesn't mean that everyone else has the same idea.

I called Jack to tell him I had resigned! He was shocked at first, but then he suggested we meet for lunch to talk things over. I told him I was planning to work as a substitute teacher, but the pay is poor and I'll get no benefits, which worries me because I have a family to look after. I was hoping he might offer me a job or be able to recommend me to one of his clients. I was surprised when he invited me to join him for lunch at the Irish Inn at Glen Echo. It's a nice, casual atmosphere with a great menu and excellent service—sort of a gastro pub, just the right place for spontaneous and relaxed discussions. Jack told me the business is going well right now. He spent yesterday in New York—just a day trip. He says he won't stay overnight in that town right now because the whole place is infested with bed bugs! When the server asked if we wanted dessert, I felt that Jack had only been half listening to me. He was making appropriate noises about how substitute teaching would be a good experience for me. I also told him I was thinking about working for the government, and he agreed that would give me better job security. I felt a little bit startled when I realized the way he was looking at me—hard to describe; it just seemed different. The server asked, again, if we wanted dessert. Jack ordered bread and butter pudding. As we left the restaurant, Jack grabbed a huge handful of chocolate mints from the reception desk and stuffed them into the pocket of his jacket.

Grace 24

Jack suggested we should take a little trip somewhere; he thought it would be good to spend time in Florida. He showed me the photos on his laptop of the hotel he had chosen. It looked absolutely gorgeous—right on the beach with nothing but silver sand and breaking waves, close to lots of shops and restaurants. Jack has never done this before; normally, he leaves all the vacation planning to me, so that was quite a surprise. The weather was kind to us, not too hot or humid. Of course, the sea breezes help. My favorite pastime was swimming in the sea. The water was so warm, and the surf breaking over my back was such a soft caress; a trick of nature since the force of the waves knocks you off balance and the rip tides are treacherous. The short vacation did wonders for both of us. We came home feeling so relaxed. It was a good way to forget what the future might hold.

Sadly, our holiday feeling didn't last long. Jack was on a conference call on the house phone. I realized I would have to put out the trash ready for collection tomorrow, so I went into Jack's study and mimed where I was going. He nodded that he understood. So I put on my shoes and opened the door. The siren

of the burglar alarm screeched through the house. I had forgotten
to switch off the alarm. I quickly keyed in the code and ran
toward Jack's study. He came out to meet me, holding the phone
in his hand. He was shaking his head and almost jumping up and
down with frustration. I apologized profusely for disturbing him.
However, I had not just disturbed him; I had cut him off from the
conference call. Needless to say, the atmosphere in the house was
chilly for several hours after that.

As we were getting ready for bed, Jack told me that Kendra
has resigned. It drives me mad that he waits until that time of
day to tell me things. Kendra is a very foolish woman! I don't
know what she's thinking about. It seems her plan is to work as a
substitute teacher. She's giving up all the benefits of working for
a reasonably sized company to earn a pittance with no benefits.
It all seems very irresponsible! I wonder if she's really going to do
that or if she wants Jack to offer her a job. Jack says it's all about
some little problem that she's got out of proportion. He told me
he took her out to lunch to give her some advice. Well, I don't
know if my memory is playing tricks on me, but I don't recall
him saying he had arranged to have lunch with her! While he
was telling me this, he was packing his stuff for another business
trip to New York. I should have done it for him yesterday, but I
was feeling exhausted.

Kendra 24

Well, I'm traumatized! I came home and just slumped on the sofa with a cup of coffee trying to take in my first experience as a substitute teacher. The phone rang at nine o'clock last night, offering me work in the special education department of a middle school in McLean. I was truly delighted to get the assignment and managed to figure out how to get there. Thankfully, it's only ten minutes drive from the apartment. I hadn't realized the assignment was only a half day's work, so I arrived there at the start of the school day. The administrator was really nice and assigned me to teach civics in the morning. I really enjoyed that! The lesson plan was easy: get the kids to read a booklet on economics and then summarize their comprehension. It was quite fascinating! The kids were fourteen years old and so well behaved. The rest of the day was rather different. After lunch, I moved to the special education classroom. It was such a relief to discover there were four classroom assistants on hand but only ten students in the class, all teenagers, all with serious learning difficulties. The most significant case was a huge fellow, thirteen years old but with a mental age of twelve months, who was unable to attend to his bathroom needs unaided; he had a classroom assistant assigned to him full time. What a humbling experience to watch the love and attention she lavished on him, fiercely protecting him from other students.

The teaching required was minimal, simply practicing handwriting and working through basic arithmetic problems. My first day on the job, and it's obviously a huge mistake! I'm not cut out for this type of thing at all. I had pinned my hopes on Jack either offering me a job or recommending me to some of his business contacts. I should never have quit working for Leo. Despair is creeping in now, but I only have myself to blame. Without thinking too much, I called Jack! I went babbling on about my life being a mess; he was very sympathetic. That's something I've never had from Stanley—never any sympathy when I've been feeling down. There I was blurting out my troubles to Jack, and he was actually listening! Stanley never listened to me; that was half the problem. He's not a bad guy. He's just not tuned into anyone else's feelings—certainly not mine. So we argued all the time. You can only take so much of that. Jack has always been easy to talk to. He finished up by saying I could call him anytime. That was an encouraging sign! Jack didn't say so, but I think he might try a bit harder to find another job for me, now he knows how desperate I'm feeling.

Grace 25

Jack always likes to look his best. He's well past his prime, but he says that doesn't mean he has to stop looking good. Yesterday, he had his teeth whitened by the dentist, using a laser treatment. When he came home, he gave me a big grin. I wondered what was pleasing him so much. Eventually, he solicited comments on his appearance. I forgot he was having the treatment done, but I really hadn't noticed that his teeth looked any whiter. I told him I couldn't see any difference, and he wasn't too impressed. He showed me the before and after photos from the dentist, insisting there was definitely a big improvement. I was quite honest with him. I told him his teeth looked just the same when he used the over-the-counter products he tried last month. Somehow, we got into a big argument; he told me I was negative all the time, that I spend my time hiding at home, building up a wrath to scold and control him. It all happened just before bedtime. We slept with our backs to each other. The tension was unbearable.

In the morning, he told me he hardly slept a wink and that it's emotionally exhausting dealing with me; he says he doesn't know what's got into me, that I used to be really sociable and now

I make excuses not to go out and avoid making arrangements to see friends. Everything he said to me was like a stab in the heart! How can he be so cruel to me? He's making no allowances whatsoever. It's just like he's forgotten that I ever told him I've got multiple sclerosis!

Jack was in a better mood when he came home this evening, but then we started arguing again; he actually called me some nasty names and told me to sleep in the spare bedroom; he even suggested that he might leave altogether. I was completely stunned! A few minutes later, he stood in front of me; he stated that all the tension just stemmed from communication problems; then he demanded a hug. We just stood in the kitchen, holding each other tight. I was clinging to him desperately. I just don't know where all Jack's angst is coming from. He's always been such an understanding man. I never thought that knowing I have multiple sclerosis would cause him so much stress; perhaps he'll be better next week. Jessica is paying us a weekend visit, so that should bring us together; there's never been any arguments with the kids around; we've always managed to maintain that level of civility and maturity.

Before we went to bed, Jack suggested that I get a dog; he says it would be good for me to have company at home when he's away on business. It's quite clear that my health issues have come at exactly the wrong time for Jack! If he never got involved in this new venture, I think he would have been much more understanding and able to spend time with me at home. It seems I'm a fly in the ointment.

Kendra 25

I'm utterly exhausted! My second time working as a substitute teacher after two failed attempts earlier this week! This is a lot more difficult than I anticipated. Each morning, I set my alarm for five o'clock. I've tried different ways of using the system. I can wait until the system phones me, but that hasn't happened since last week when I worked in special education. I'm never doing that again! I'm just not cut out for dealing with that kind of challenge. So I took myself out of the phone system. I decided I would control the system rather than the other way around. So when my alarm clock goes off, I leap out of bed and try the system. I log onto my profile online, make myself available for work, and check the system for possible assignments. The result: nothing, nothing, nothing. All very disheartening! In between times, I get myself ready for action. Shower. Try the system. Get dressed. Try the system. Put makeup on. Try the system. Prepare lunches for me and the kids. Try the system. Rouse the kids for school. Try the system. Make breakfast for the kids. Try the system again. By that time, it's six o'clock. I tried the other way of using the system—phoning the help desk to find same-day jobs, but I can hardly hear what she's saying because she talks so fast. The only jobs available are always too far away! I'm only allowed forty-five minutes to get there. Morning traffic limits the possibilities. So for the past two days, I've been moping at home with nothing to do but clean the apartment, do the laundry, and check online for suitable rental properties. That's another story. Rents keep coming down, so I'm holding back.

Anyway, back to yesterday. I finally got an assignment, after going through the usual routine, for an elementary teacher at a school just ten minutes drive away. I got there, all perky and ready for work. The assistant looked at me blankly when I arrived. She had cancelled the job. Another teacher was filling the slot. I told her I was sick to my stomach, so she took pity on me and quickly found me something else. My assignment would be teaching art to first and third graders. I found the classroom was locked and there was no lesson plan. I tracked down another art teacher who suggested I use one of her projects, so I found myself explaining art nouveau to these little children. I did get them to produce artwork using patterns and textures, so it was all very pleasant. But that was in the morning. In the afternoon, while I was snatching ten minutes to eat lunch, the administrator called me into the office. I would have to do some filing as well as sorting the mail. That didn't feel so good. Junior office work after I quit a well-paid executive assistant position. I left the building in the afternoon, clutching my yellow time report. I just worked for little more than minimum wage, with no benefits and no work for tomorrow! I needed someone to talk to, so I called Jack and blurted out all my problems. After he listened patiently, I said I was sorry for bothering him, but he said he was pleased to hear from me. As before, he said I could call him anytime!

Grace 26

I feel just awful. I have no energy, and my head feels kind of numb. We did attend a function last night, but I didn't drink any alcohol. The specialist's advice was to stay off alcohol, so I've followed his guidance. The event was a formal ball; normally not my favorite way to spend an evening. I was quite apprehensive because I was surrounded by a whole lot of Jack's new business associates—people I'd never met before.

While we were enjoying dinner, there were a lot of rambling speeches. I have absolutely no idea who the speakers were, since we were all trying to get acquainted with each other and nobody was listening to the speakers. The live band, after dinner, was good—two singers with really unique voices surrounded by talented musicians. I told Jack I wouldn't be able to dance. I can't trust my balance these days. So everyone danced the night away while I watched the action. I told everyone I had broken my toe; it's nobody else's business that I've got multiple sclerosis. Anyway, I did enjoy the food last night, which was wonderful. There must have been around a thousand people at the event; how the caterers managed to produce such delicate and beautifully presented dishes at the right temperature is quite beyond me. Maybe Jack could use those caterers at my funeral.

It was a bit of an effort being sociable last night. On my mind, all the time, was my conversation with Jessica; there has been no opportunity to tell her face-to-face about my multiple sclerosis, so I had to call her. I thought Jack would tell Jessica, but he didn't suggest calling her, and I didn't want to ask him to be the bearer of bad news; it would have been nice, though, if he could have explained everything to her. There's never a good time to talk to Jessica; I caught her as she was walking from the office to her car; she only had a few minutes to talk. I had to go headlong into giving her my news; she didn't say very much apart from, "Oh, no, Mom, this is terrible news." She did ask how I was feeling today and said she would come and see me soon. I told Jessica about the dreams I was having about her. There was a long silence at the end of the line; she didn't say anything. We finished up by her promising to visit by the end of this month. There's something going on with Jessica. I just know it!

Kendra 26

What a day! I set the alarm for four o'clock this morning. I needed to get the kids' lunch boxes ready and check their homework before trying to find an assignment. I tried the online system every ten minutes, as well as using the phone access system from five o'clock, but got absolutely nothing! At six o'clock, I accepted a two-day assignment at an elementary school in Vienna. What a relief! A two-day assignment means I don't need to get up so early tomorrow to find work.

I was delighted with the detailed lesson plan, but it sent my head spinning. Eyes down! Stay calm! Work out how to operate the television, the DVD player, the overhead projector, and find all the books and practice papers for math and science. I had to teach the kids how to multiply and divide in decimals as well as conduct a science lesson on the difference between sunlight, moonlight, and artificial light. The next thing I know, the door opens and the principal tells me the lesson plan is wrong. We need to leave, right away, on a field trip. We attended a rehearsal of Shakespeare's *As You Like It* at a local theater. The kids couldn't understand very much, but the object of the exercise was to show them how to behave at a theatrical performance.

Back in the class, I had an incident with two boys. One hit the other, by accident; the other boy reacted by kicking him in the groin. We openly discussed their behavior, and they both apologized, very sincerely. At the end of the day, I discussed the incident with the principal. I got so involved in the matter that I didn't realize I had spent an hour in the office! Thankfully, Stanley had agreed to pick the kids up from school; otherwise, I would have had serious problems at home.

I thought Stanley would, at least, show some interest in my new line of work! No chance! All he was interested in was getting away, as fast as possible. Su tells me he has promised her a new car—not brand new, but almost new. It sounds great with only a few miles on the clock; he says she'll get the car any day now.

Just as I was preparing dinner for the kids, Jack phoned. I was hoping he had a job interview for me, but he was calling to see if I was all right. He said he was quite worried about me. I was distracted, so we spent just a few minutes talking. I told him today was a better day and not to worry about me. I wonder if I'm giving Jack the wrong signals. Maybe he thinks I'm chasing after him. I'll have to make sure he doesn't get the wrong impression!

Grace 27

Jack was not in a very good mood last night; he had hoped the federal loan for Spelectra would be matched by private investors, which would help create thousands of jobs; however, some kind of legal problem has emerged, so he spent most of the evening in the study poring over documents. I was looking forward to telling Jack all about my day, but he was preoccupied with his business issues.

I've been housebound for days. I just don't have the energy to join Miriam and the hiking group in the mornings, and my gym membership has been a waste of time. On my calendar, yesterday, was the annual lunch for the Donagh Foundation; I decided to make the effort and attend the event. It took so long to get myself ready, I almost called off. Everyone has been very understanding about me stepping back in recent months; the word is out about my health issues—news travels fast. I was the greatest thing since sliced bread for a long time at the Foundation; then I got taken for granted, but that's how it goes. I really had no thoughts of attending the lunch, but the president called me with entreaties that everyone would love to see me there; she even offered to collect me so that I didn't have to drive. My confidence behind

the wheel has gone downhill since my diagnosis, I must admit;
I feel my reactions are slower; I seem to have a lot of people
honking their horns at me whenever I venture out.

So I reluctantly agreed to go to the lunch; she arrived in her
car with a bunch of ladies who were all very concerned about the
weather; we had driving rain all through the night and a tornado
watch this morning. Miraculously, we got there safely, only half
an hour later than planned, so all we missed was the reception
with a member of Congress giving an address about education;
I wanted to hear the speech but might be able to get hold of
a transcript.

We didn't need to worry about seating arrangements since
we all know each other well. Unfortunately, the lunch was
fairly appalling; such delightful ladies; not a single complaint;
everyone silently thinking it was a good excuse to keep the calorie
intake down. Coffee arrived, and we sat back to enjoy the main
speaker—a female comedienne from Canada. Everyone was
chuckling with laughter; then, surprisingly, she came down from
the stage and mingled with the audience, approaching each table
and making really bitchy comments about everyone's outfits; you
could feel the tension level increase and a feeling of dread mixed
with the laughter as she approached our table.

Suddenly, I could hear my name mentioned. I couldn't
understand what was going on. Next thing, I was asked to
take the stage. The club president was handing me an award...
appreciation of all my hard work for the organization over the last
ten years. I was completely stunned...but what a good feeling...
I was just glowing with delight. It's a huge crystal bowl with my
name engraved on it just below the name of the Foundation.
When I got home, I put the award in plain sight in the kitchen
so that Jack couldn't miss it. Jack noticed the crystal bowl as soon
as he came in; he was very pleased that I had been recognized and
told me he was proud of me. It feels good to have my self-esteem
raised and to feel a worthy partner for Jack.

Kendra 27

Another day as a substitute teacher! I'm so thankful today was a pre-arranged assignment. I'm beginning to feel quite buoyant about the whole scene. I've struck up a good relationship with several schools. It means I don't have to get up at five in the morning to find work. So this morning was sheer luxury, especially since the school is only five minutes away. It's an elementary school with a start time of eight o'clock, so it means I can get the kids out the door before me. Sheer heaven!

The only problem with all of this change of circumstances is that Aidan's behavior is giving me cause for concern. Last night, I received a phone call from his school principal. Apparently, he hit another boy with a chair while the teacher's back was turned! The teacher immediately arranged for him to meet with a counselor on the same day. It seems that the lack of a father figure in his life is the crux of the problem. He told the counselor that he never knows when he'll see his father and whenever he does see him, there's no opportunity to talk to him—it's just a few hours of being allowed a special treat. He actually told the counselor that he needs strong control! What can I do about this? My son needs a role model in his life. He needs someone who can give him advice on how to handle everything that comes his way—name calling from other children, physical attacks from other boys, help with his homework. He needs a male figure in his life. He needs someone who will take him to ball games. He needs someone to show him how to be a man. The father figure in this boy's life is like being in the movie theater. It's unreal, only lasts for a few hours, and there's only one-way communication.

Stanley just doesn't have the stomach to be a parent! He never asks about anything. He just takes him out in the car with the music blaring, drives him to a movie theater or a theme park or some other form of entertainment, and then drops him off back home. Once he leaves, he just moves on and doesn't give Aidan another thought until the next pre-arranged visit.

Tamara is so cute; she makes up for all the problems. Six years old is such a lovely age! Last night, she found a stink bug and asked if she could open the window to set it free. I told her the correct thing to do is use a tissue and flush it down the toilet. She opened her hand to show me the bug. It did look so defenseless cupped in her hand, with its delicate legs tickling her palm. I explained that if we set it free, it would just go out and make a lot more stink bugs. I had to explain that those bugs are pests and need to be controlled; her little face crumpled. The tears were due any second, so I relented. She looked so peaceful and happy when the insect was released. It did make me wonder about killing God's creatures.

Grace 28

I had hoped to feel strong enough to hike with Miriam this morning, but the alarm went off just after Jack had gone to work—not the burglar alarm but the septic tank alarm. The noise was deafening, going on and off every few minutes; I had no idea how to turn the thing off. I scrambled around and found the telephone number for the septic tank people; they have no idea when they can get here, sometime today, they said. I've had shooting pains in my head and my legs for two days, and I'm feeling exhausted. That alarm going off this morning has made me feel very stressed. I'm finding I need to stay tranquil and not get into situations that will make me uptight. Once I get stressed, it seems to take days to wear off.

As I was getting myself dressed, my hand swiped a bottle of nail polish that crashed onto the tiled floor in the bathroom. I couldn't believe the mess—nail polish all over the floor and all down the side of my clothes; glass scattered everywhere. I'm so glad Jack wasn't here to witness this scene. What would be his reaction as he looked at his ailing wife whose trembling hands had spoiled everything? I can just picture the look on his face as he imagined the years rolling on with my symptoms getting steadily worse.

Jack mentioned Kendra's birthday again. Usually I arrange a gift, but I told Jack I wasn't going to do it. I don't have the energy to go trailing round the shops, so he said he would do it himself; he can surely arrange a delivery of flowers.

Jack told me, as he was leaving this morning, that Jessica had called him from Boston; she's planning to visit soon. I don't know why she didn't call me; after all, I'm sitting at home with no one to talk to. Maybe she thinks I'll keep her talking too long; she's always so caught up with work...deadlines and so on. I'm still having that dream about Jessica.

I feel empty...my life has no purpose... Jack doesn't need me. There's no hope of a family wedding or any grandchildren to give joy to our lives...neither Jessica nor Edward show any signs of creating a home that Jack and I could, perhaps, occupy in our elderly years. I don't know where I'm going to end up if I'm not able to walk or take care of myself.

Kendra 28

I decided to give Jack a call. He did call me last time, so it's not like I'm chasing him. He said he wished I had a better exit strategy when I quit my job. He kind of hinted that I was a bit foolish. He mentioned pride and resentment, but not a direct criticism. Somehow Jack can get his message across without making you feel bad! He did say what I need is a secure position with a well-established organization. He's been trying to recruit a new secretary, but he hasn't interviewed anyone he wants to hire. That was news to me.

The school system has gone haywire! I received two automated calls last night offering me assignments. Each time, I pressed the button to hear more. I didn't want the jobs. One school was too far away. The other assignment was on a day I can't work because I have a doctor's appointment. That's another thing about being a substitute. I lose a whole day's work if I have medical or dental appointments. I can't cancel the assignments because that would give me a bad record. Now I need to phone the central office to tell them I've got technical problems with the system. The first problem is for a date next week; that means I can't search for assignments for that date until I get this cleared up. The other date is six weeks away, so there's time to resolve this. As if I don't have enough to do, I have to unravel this mess.

My bedroom is in chaos! The floor is covered with paperwork, unread newspapers, unopened mail, and envelopes that have been opened with no action on the contents. Piles of stuff have been mounting up for weeks. Everything is out of control!

Jack called to wish me happy birthday for tomorrow! I was surprised he remembered. I was even more surprised when he told me he got me a gift! He said he went into Williams Sonoma at Tyson's Corner and bought me a huge bag of goodies, all kinds of wonderful foodie items I would never buy for myself, but he knows I'll love them. He said Grace isn't fit for shopping. Now that she has multiple sclerosis, she's too exhausted. I found myself suggesting that he and Grace come over for dinner, but he said Grace isn't really fit for social occasions now. Jack said he would call me again. He wants to deliver my birthday gift over the weekend.

Grace 29

I'm feeling so bad. I didn't get a wink of sleep last night. I walked around the neighborhood with Miriam and the hiking girls this morning. I desperately, needed some company. I knew I wouldn't be able to keep up with them, but they're so understanding. We went once around the neighborhood at a slow pace. I gave up as we came past our house again. They waved as they walked on. I watched as they picked up speed. How I wish I could have my energy back again and do all the things I used to do.

Jack is always complaining that I keep interrupting him. My complaint is that he takes up all the air time. He appears to listen, but he doesn't really want to hear about my day. Somehow, I always feel cheated. I do more listening than him, but he says I'm the one who doesn't listen. That kind of comment really gets under my skin. Last night, he kept talking about the market conditions in the industry. He's worried that China is producing conventional solar modules at such a low cost and his new technology won't be able to compete. I was actively listening because I desperately want to know what's going on in Jack's life. Suddenly, he told me to stop interrupting him. I was stung because I hadn't said a word. Well, we had rather a chilly evening. I spent several hours watching television while he pored over a whole bunch of reports. As we were getting ready for bed, Jack told me he needs some excitement in his life. He complained that I never want to go anywhere. He wants to plan a trip to Australia and New Zealand, but I told him my days of long-haul traveling are over. I suggested going to Boston for the weekend to see Jessica, but he says it's easier for her to travel here.

Jack left this morning for a trip to San Diego. With a long day ahead of me, I decided to return a shirt I bought at the Galleria. I quite liked it, until I saw a wrinkly old woman wearing the very same thing. I decided to use Jack's car. Rain was threatened, so I put my rain jacket in the trunk of the car. Inside the trunk was a huge bag full of gourmet cooking ingredients! There must be several hundred dollars of spices and sauces in that bag. I called Jack to ask him about the bag. He was quite taken aback. "Oh, you found it," he said "It was supposed to be a surprise. I thought it might renew your interest in gourmet cooking." I was really touched. Jack said he thought it might inspire me to come up with recipe ideas for Jessica's visit.

Kendra 29

Last night, I got three phone calls from the automated system with job offers I didn't want. The first offered two hours teaching English, the next offered three hours teaching kindergarten, and the last was teaching music. I took a gamble and turned down all the assignments. I held out until the help desk opened at six o'clock, holding on the line for almost half an hour. I turned on the speaker phone and packed the kids' lunch boxes, made a flask of coffee, emptied the dishwasher, and made scrambled eggs for breakfast. I'm pretty good at multitasking!

My tenacity paid off! Teaching art in Vienna was my prize! I had a wonderful day! I would have paid an entrance fee for today. It was loads of fun. I got the kids making prints by carving rubber squares. I also had the younger kids designing a holiday card to send to their friends and family. In the afternoon, we attended a performance in the assembly hall, given by a mime artist. The reaction from the kids was a treat. They were all screaming and whistling with delight and stamping their feet. The object of the exercise was to socialize them in those kinds of situations. By the end, these kids were so good, politely applauding like little grown-ups.

Being back in the school environment has made me think of the early years of my marriage. Life is really hard at the moment, not to mention the loneliness. If my marriage hadn't failed, I would be living in a decent house without any money worries. I started thinking about the high hopes I had for life with Stanley. He's not a bad guy. He just never managed to be a good provider, not to mention being unreliable! We're still waiting for him to deliver that car for Su! What a fool I was to get married so young! Married at eighteen with my first kid at nineteen was just asking for trouble! I really thought I could go it alone and be one of those self-sufficient single parents, but it's really, really hard. There's just no respite from the responsibility!

I need a man in my life! But how am I going to make that happen? I really need to think about online dating, but it's too scary meeting up with total strangers. I wonder if Jack knows any nice men who are available. Any one of his business contacts would be a great catch for me. I need an older man who would be prepared to take on three children. Not many of them around! Maybe Jack could set me up with someone who is kind, understanding, and financially secure.

Grace 30

I don't know why I seem to get nothing accomplished. Today was a totally free day; all I had to do was catch up on chores. Somehow I'm further behind than I was at the beginning of the day. Everything is in a mess. My study is full of papers that need attention; everywhere I look is covered in dust, and every room is untidy. Losing Carmellita was quite a blow. It's hard to come to terms with this situation. Giving a statement to the police was quite nerve wracking.

A few days ago, Miriam asked if I had noticed anything gone missing; some items had disappeared from her home, and she suspected our shared housekeeper was the culprit. I just couldn't believe that could possibly be true. Miriam said what alerted her was some items appeared in her home that didn't belong to her, and then she realized that some of her own stuff was missing. She entreated me to come into her house and see if I recognized any of the items that had materialized around her home. I was amazed to recognize some of our belongings. We drove straight to the housekeeper's apartment for a confrontation. Her husband answered the door. Carmellita was not at home. We asked if we could step inside. We were both stunned into silence the minute the door closed. All around us, like the contents of Aladdin's cave, were our belongings. Miriam used her iPod to take photos of everything. I called Carmellita on her cell phone. Somehow, my stress turned to anger, and I screamed down the phone at her. On the other end of the phone, all I could hear was wailing. That was three days ago. Now, her husband says she has returned to Guatemala. Well, she won't get back into the United States, but that won't bring back our stolen belongings, nor will it restore my trust in human nature. We treated Carmellita very well, and she betrayed us. We only have ourselves to blame for giving her too much opportunity to steal from us. It's just so depressing.

I needed to unburden myself, so I called Jessica but just got her answering machine. I called Edward next; he was sympathetic, dear boy; he says he'll come and see me tomorrow. I haven't seen Edward since he told me about his relationship with Rodrigo. I told him he needs to stay for dinner tomorrow evening; that will give him an opportunity to tell his dad. Jack wasn't too bothered about the Carmellita situation; he just says I should find someone to replace her. What Jack doesn't understand is Carmellita was used to my ways; she knew how I like things done. I don't have the energy to train someone else. Well, Edward and Jack will have to turn a blind eye to the lack of housekeeping. I want to make a special dinner for my boys.

Kendra 30

I actually managed to work four days this week! I'm getting a little more savvy every time! Yesterday morning, I called the system at five o'clock. The only thing going was for grade six at an elementary school in Reston, so I took it. The lesson plan highlighted that one boy needed special attention. Sure enough, this boy was playing up right from the start; he slammed his books down and was loud and aggressive to the other kids. During the first hour, he was talking and sniggering. Instead of moving him, I moved the others away until he was isolated. He pulled his sweatshirt up over his head. After ten minutes, the sweatshirt came down and he carried on with his work. I crouched down beside him and whispered, "I think you're seeking attention. Am I right?" To my surprise, he answered, "Yes." I asked him "Is that because you're not getting attention at home?" Again, he replied "Yes." I questioned, "Who is at home with you?" I discovered there is no father at home. "So you're the man of the house," I tell him. "Does your mom work really hard?" He answered, "Yes." So I pushed a little further, "When you grow up, would you like to earn a lot of money so that your mom won't have to work so hard?" Again, he answered "Yes." So I asked him

"How can you achieve that?" He thought for a long time and answered, "I have to study." I smiled. "You're a smart boy. In fact, I think you might be the cleverest boy in the class. What do you think?" He tried hard not to smile. "Maybe," he answered. "Okay," I told him. "I want to see your behavior improve." He looked at me, with interest. "Why all the questions?" he wanted to know. "Because I like you," I answered and moved away.

I couldn't believe the transformation. Instead of being the class troublemaker, this boy turned into the class president, telling the other kids to be quiet and keeping everyone in line when moving to lunch and to recess. I so enjoyed my day with the class. I'm amazed to find that I'm actually quite good at teaching. It's just an extension of being a mother, really. This boy has the same issues as Aidan! No father at home, so I have to perform both roles. It's not good! If Aidan doesn't get a strong male role model in his life, I'm going to have more problems down the road.

Today, I'm not working; a birthday treat for myself! I was looking forward to using the gourmet gift from Jack, but he said he changed his mind and gave it to Grace. I was disappointed because I was looking forward to seeing him. He told me he had a better idea! He was sending me two tickets for the Washington Ballet performance of *Romeo and Juliet*. I squealed with delight at the idea of an expensive theater ticket. "For you and a friend," he told me. I found myself answering, "Well, you're my friend, aren't you?"

Grace 31

Jack was entertaining some private investors from California over the weekend; they were over here for a business convention and wanted to do some tourist trips. I suggested to Jack that Edward could join them for some male company, but, somehow, our son didn't get to tag along. Jack's entourage went to Gettysburg for the day, all boys' stuff—battlefields, guns, and monuments.

I have to admit I was glad to get Jack out of my hair; he's driving me crazy right now. Somehow he never seems to enjoy anything; if we go anywhere, he complains about the traffic and shouts at other drivers. At a restaurant, he is rude to the waiters and never enjoys his meal. If he can't find fault with the food, he decides he's made the wrong choice and orders something else; consequently, two half-eaten meals are thrown in the trash. I don't know how he turned into a grumpy old man; he was always the life and soul of the party when we were young.

I decided to make soup while I had a peaceful Saturday to myself. I always make good use of vegetables from the garden. By the time I peeled the vegetables and cut everything into chunks, my hands were really aching. Not only did my hands ache, but I had strange feelings in my feet—stinging sensations on my heels, and the bones on my ankles felt like they had been tied with rope.

The men were delighted with my carrot and orange soup when they returned from the battlefields of Gettysburg; it did taste so good; decorated with a blob of sour cream and surrounded by croutons, it looked very appealing. I'm just sorry I didn't look appealing. I look more like an old witch every day. I actually feel that Jack was ashamed of me this weekend. I felt embarrassed all the time his guests were here. In the past, I would have been all dressed up, the house would be looking good, and I would be lively company for Jack and his guests.

Now, the house looks neglected, I'm wearing comfortable clothes, and my whole persona is lethargic and dull. Jack said he wants to start searching for a full-time caregiver to look after me. What kind of person is that? Some total stranger in my home who will wash and dress me and make the meals? What kind of person wants to do a job like that? I don't need looking after. I can look after myself. I don't want strangers in my house.

What do I have to look forward to? It doesn't look as if Edward or Jessica will ever provide me with grandchildren, and Jack is more devoted to Spelectra than he is to me!

Kendra 31

Yesterday I was the substitute teacher at an elementary school in Vienna. I had my hands full this time! One boy flushed the toilet of the en-suite bathroom every few minutes, while another boy just could not sit still or stop talking. I managed to keep everything going during the math lesson but found my temper rising as I pointed a finger and raised my voice. I realized I was about to lose my cool. I caught myself quickly and spoke soothingly to the boy. What a transformation! Suddenly, he became a totally different character, quiet and eager to please.

After showing a video about explorers in North America, I encouraged the students to dance to the music that accompanied the credits. Big mistake! The children became utterly wild. One boy threw himself across the desks, while other children were climbing onto the desks. The noise level became hysterical. I blew the whistle that I always keep in my pocket for emergencies and got the classroom under control quickly. That was a big lesson for me! When you have kids sitting quietly, keep them that way! I appointed the biggest troublemaker as line leader on our way to the cafeteria and kept rewarding him for any remote sign of good behavior. My strategy worked. At the end of the day, the two problem kids told me I was a very nice teacher and asked if I could come back tomorrow.

In the office, I discovered that two boys in the class have attention deficit disorder, one has Asperger's, and five others are suffering from emotional disturbance! I'm truly astonished that I was thrown into the lion's den without any of that information!

Such a day kept me from thinking about Jack and our evening together at the ballet. If I could meet a man like Jack, I would be so happy. The ballet was amazing! I was completely spellbound! The performance was a testament to the civilization of the human race; the scenery was awesome, the costumes were spectacular, and the supporting actors and chorus were mesmerizing. As the curtain fell on the first act, I made no eye contact with Jack. We moved out to the foyer of the Kennedy Center, self-consciously admiring the posters for forthcoming events. Returning to our seats, we exchanged a few whispered words before the curtain came up on Act Two. I choked back tears as Romeo killed Tybalt and was banished from Verona forever. As the curtain rose on Juliet's bedchamber in Act Three, I envisaged Juliet stabbing herself and Romeo in the final scene. I felt very agitated and couldn't concentrate on the performance. I thought about touching Jack's hand. I left my seat and watched the finale from the back of the theater. I feel so stupid! I let my emotions run away with me at the theater. Somehow, I need to thank Jack for my birthday gift and apologize for disappearing. I'll make some excuse about not feeling well.

Grace 32

Yesterday was our wedding anniversary. Jack arranged for us to have lunch at the Towers Club. There was a card and flowers waiting for me in the kitchen in the morning. Another envelope held two tickets for *Hair*, which was showing at the Opera House in the Kennedy Center. There was a message inside the envelope from Jack saying he couldn't make the performance tonight due to a business commitment, but I should invite a friend. I was disappointed but intrigued to see the show again; I saw it on Broadway when it opened, years ago, and loved it. I gave Miriam a call; she was delighted at the opportunity to accompany me and agreed to drive. I can't trust myself to drive farther than the grocery store these days.

I don't know how I sat through that show with Miriam. I found myself rejecting all of the values. I found the nudity pathetic and the promiscuity demeaning and disgusting. I totally reject the drug culture, which is nothing but an evil influence on society, and I have no tolerance for laziness and the lack of work ethic. Furthermore, apart from one number, the music in the show was so forgettable. I have no idea why this kind of thing appealed to me all those years ago. The rebellion of youth, I suppose.

Lunch with Jack was pleasant, but he was very distracted, taking calls on his cell phone all the time. We're not getting along well, at all, at the moment. He's behaving like a teenager whose hormones are out of balance, so I've started treating him that way; it's the only peaceful solution.

I've noticed Jack has stopped telling me he loves me. Whenever he goes out, I say good-bye to him, but he doesn't answer; he just looks at me with a defiant glare. He actually leaves the house on weekends without telling me where he's going; I'm supposed to guess that he's gone to the office or the gym or the grocery store or the mall. We're on dangerous ground, I fear, so my tactic is to overcompensate for his behavior. I've been buying him little gifts and leaving them on his chair—a new tie, a pair of sunglasses, a bottle of his favorite wine. I hope we can have a better atmosphere at home soon. It's always the woman who has to set the tone at home. If Jack's business problems are so bad they're causing him to behave like this, then maybe he should give up the whole venture. What kind of future did Jack envisage for himself before all these changes in our lives? He expected he would retire and enjoy his golf membership at River Bend. We could travel together. He assumed that grandchildren would follow, once either Edward or Jessica settled down and got married. Jack expected to look forward to some relaxing and carefree years ahead. What has he got instead? A business venture that's swallowed his capital and fast running into trouble, along with an invalid wife and no hope of grandchildren.

Kendra 32

I called Jack to thank him. I waited until midmorning. He didn't say much, just, "Good to hear from you. I'll call you later." I rehearsed what I wanted to say to him. I kept my tone light, apologized for running out of the theater before the end of the performance, gave the excuse about not feeling well, and thanked him for his generous birthday gift. I made sure not to give him any encouragement. It seems to have worked. I feel so sad that Grace has multiple sclerosis. She'll need Jack by her side.

So I have teaching to keep my mind off Jack! Today was a dream day at an elementary school in Herndon. I had a class of normal children. Well, almost normal. The schedule started with math. We worked on estimated fractions. I explained the concept and asked the children to work on fifteen questions. In a twinkling of an eye, a little boy seated right in front of my desk had completed his task with every single answer correct and was working on a puzzle on the floor. Gently, I asked him to return to his desk. He wailed and cried and refused to move. Meanwhile, the other children were pondering the answer to the second question. Each lesson was the same; he finished in a twinkle and sat on the floor with his puzzle. During social studies, the children had to write six questions they would ask a famous explorer in an interview. Again, he was finished and sitting on the floor with his puzzle. This time, I saw he had not completed his task. I crouched beside him and suggested he go back to his desk and finish his work. His response was to wail and bawl loudly. He held his head in his hands and yelled that he could only think of two questions to ask the explorer. I gave him a suggestion, and he immediately quieted down and scribbled furiously. Another child with issues! I do think it would be sensible to be prewarned about these children! Suddenly, a voice boomed into the classroom. An administrator asked me to send the attendance list to the office. The children yelled back that the messenger had delivered this at the beginning of the day. What a surprise for me to find out there's a speaker on the ceiling. Now I discover that every interaction in my classroom can be monitored! It's a good thing, but it would have been nice to know!

It's past bedtime, and my family is asleep. The apartment is quiet, except for the noise coming from the footsteps of the upstairs residents and the passing traffic outside. I need to stop thinking about Jack. I need to get my life in order. I need to find a better place to live. I need to find a job that pays a decent salary. And Stanley needs to be a better father figure. I'm still angry with him. He promised Su a new car. Weeks have passed, and now he tells me he doesn't have the money! He really is useless!

Grace 33

When I woke up this morning, I had difficulty getting out of bed. I pushed myself up on my elbows, but I could barely hold that position. I tried to roll over so that my feet were dangling out of the bed, but I couldn't make that happen. I did manage to roll over onto my side, but I couldn't make my legs move. My legs felt paralyzed. I tried again, several times, but each time I got more exhausted. I tried resting for a few minutes, but the same thing happened. I tried to yell for Jack, but I couldn't raise my voice loud enough to be heard. Eventually, I managed to roll over onto my stomach and reach down for a book, which was lying on the floor beside the bed. I used the hardback book to make thumping noises on the wooden headboard above the bed.

After a few minutes, Jack appeared, looking alarmed. "I can't get out of bed," I whispered. He looked relieved. "I wondered what all the noise was about. I thought the furnace was playing up," was his response. Leaning on Jack's arm while he dragged me to the edge of the bed, I realized how long it's been since we had the slightest physical contact. Jack got me standing on my feet, but I couldn't stay upright without holding his arm. He left me sitting on the bed and came back with a golfing umbrella. "Lean on that," he instructed. I managed to shuffle to the stairs and, holding onto the railings, got myself down to the kitchen, where Jack was eating yoghurt at the breakfast bar. Jack glanced up as he answered his cell phone. He smiled. "Good to hear from you," I heard him say, followed by, "I'll call you later." As he looked back at me, his smile disappeared. "Who was that?" I asked. "Kendra," he answered, looking down again. "What does she want?" His gaze met mine, but his eyes were empty. "She's looking for work."

After Jack left, I sat staring into space for a long time... I feel like I'm looking at my future through a shattered pane of glass... I always looked at the future through an open window before...a window with a clear view of sunshine. Now that window has been slammed shut.

Kendra 33

Jack called me back this afternoon! He wanted to meet for coffee, so I asked him to drop by the apartment. As the kids were doing their homework around the dining table, we just chatted about general things. Jack asked about my day, so I went into full throttle, telling him that I've got a good relationship with the school administrators. I call the schools direct each week. That way I get good assignments rather than waiting for a phone call at five o'clock in the morning. Jack showed great interest in how things were going. It was so exhilarating to be able to tell someone about my day and to realize they were actually listening. Stanley never showed much interest in what I had been doing during the day. His main interest was what was on the menu for dinner. So I told Jack that today at the middle school where I was supposed to be teaching English, I was disappointed to discover I wouldn't be doing any actual teaching, just showing a DVD and ensuring that students completed the worksheet. I told him that my report at the end of the day contained two issues. I noticed that one girl's head was bent very low over her desk. She had written almost nothing on her worksheet but had managed to write a full-page letter to a friend. The contents of the letter were sexually explicit. At the end of the period, I advised that her regular teacher would probably involve her in a discussion. At lunchtime, I showed the letter to the school counselor, who described the content of the letter as not appropriate for a girl of her age. Not appropriate for any age! The very idea that my teenage daughter might write something like that is totally sickening!

Jack commented that I seemed to be enjoying teaching, despite this morning's issue. To keep him entertained, I told him about my last class of the day when one boy's pen exploded, spattering ink all over his desk and onto the classroom wall. He managed to clean his desk, but his cleaning efforts made a bigger mess on the wall. So I gave him two assignments. He needs to write an essay on the science of stain removal and bring appropriate cleaning materials tomorrow for a further attempt at cleaning the wall. I told Jack that I felt no satisfaction at my day's work. All I've done is make chump change. Jack nodded and said he would look into getting me a proper job.

It was comfortable chatting to Jack. Out in the hallway, as he was leaving, I apologized again for leaving the theater early and thanked him for such a thoughtful birthday gift. Jack held my hand and gently kissed my cheek. "Let's do it again," he said. I stood at the doorway, watching him leave. As he reached his car, he turned around. I raised my hand, and he smiled as he opened the car door.

Grace 34

I got over my "episode" in three days. I never want to go through that again. The doctor did warn me this would probably happen. I think this means there's no doubt about the diagnosis of MS; the "episode" is confirmation. Jack has been very practical; he arranged for Jessica and Edward to visit for the weekend, and he asked Miriam to keep checking on me today. He's planning to hire someone to be at home with me full time. I don't want to lead this kind of life—it's pointless. It might be different if Jack hadn't changed so much. My diagnosis seems to have changed his feelings. There's a coldness toward me; he sleeps in another room; he checks that I'm still alive in the morning, and then I don't see or hear from him during the day.

Once I'm able to drive again, I have a special purpose in mind. I've decided to organize my own funeral. We don't use our membership at River Bend very much, but it's the perfect venue. Jack would never be able to organize things properly, so it's best if I plan well ahead. This afternoon, I spoke to the banqueting manager on the pretext that I wanted to organize a fundraising event. I'll have to choose between the ballroom or one of the function rooms. The ballroom holds three hundred people, and the function room can cope with seventy people. I discussed menus and prices, as well as facilities for speech making—microphone, podium, etc. I'll make a folder with all my preferences and leave it on the desk in my study. Jack could simply call River Bend and follow my instructions.

I also want to update my will. The will is quite old, and life has moved on so much. Jack's will makes me sick; he has left bequests of really large sums to three useless nephews. These young men totally ignored Jack in the past when he had his heart attack—not a phone call, not a card, not a letter, nothing. I just can't fathom Jack's thinking; it seems he's trying to persuade people to mourn his passing. The truth is these nephews haven't given him a passing thought in years. My half share of the house will go to Jack, the contents of the house to Miriam, my jewelry to Jessica, and my shares to Edward.

I keep having the same dream about Jessica. She's in a pond of muddy water, reaching out to me, but I'm powerless to help her. I've never had recurring dreams before; this has to mean something. Jessica was very quiet over the weekend while she was here; she was very subdued, as if she had something on her mind. She was very attentive and loving, always running around after me, but there's something not right.

Kendra 34

I just discovered the hourly rate for housekeepers! It's almost double what I earn from teaching! And housekeepers get holiday gifts as well as falling heir to discarded designer outfits without having to deal with discipline problems or cope with challenging academic situations. Oh well, nothing for it but to soldier on. I'm still waiting for all those employment agencies to find me an interview, but there's not much hope on the horizon.

Today, I was teaching art at an elementary school in McLean. No lesson plan from the teacher, who had taken ill, so I had to improvise. I asked the first class to draw a winter holiday scene. No one could think of anything much besides Santa Claus, so I got them thinking about other images. I was disappointed with the behavior; the best artist in the class repeatedly drew images for other students, who tried to pass them off as their own. When the grade teacher arrived to collect her class, I informed her of my disappointment at the unacceptable behavior. The dear girl was crestfallen. She immediately informed the class that those responsible would lose recess and would be writing letters of apology to me and to their parents. Learning from this experience,

I decided the students weren't energized enough, so I changed the theme for subsequent classes to an art competition. Just the word *competition* had them buzzing with excitement. At the end of the lesson, I chose the top five pictures and instructed the class to vote for the best. Each winning student was overjoyed with the recognition. At the end of the day, the offending students from this morning delivered their letters of apology to me and apologized verbally in a very contrite fashion. I smiled broadly when reading the letters.

Jack called to suggest taking the kids for a day out on the weekend. He suggested a trip to Harpers Ferry since it's picturesque and steeped in history. It was difficult to resist, particularly since I could use the field trip for history lessons. I remembered that Harpers Ferry witnessed the first application of interchangeable parts, the arrival of the first successful American railroad, John Brown's attack on slavery, and the largest surrender of Federal troops during the Civil War. It would be a great family outing. But we're not a family!

I expressed my misgivings to Jack, but he said it's just an innocent day out. I asked Jack about Grace, but he said she's not fit for long car journeys right now. I read out some of the apology letters from the art students this morning. Jack was chuckling away. It was so comforting being able to share my day with Jack. He said it was good to hear some lighthearted talk. I'm concerned that all is not well at Spelectra. Jack told me he discovered that millions of dollars are being wasted by technicians dumping brand new glass tubes (which could have been used on subsequent installations) into dumpsters. As we finished telling each other our woes, Jack arranged to meet us in Harpers Ferry on Saturday.

Grace 35

Jack made me listen to details of investments he made, this evening… I'm just not into finance, but I listened, patiently… I did ask some questions because I didn't fully understand. However, Jack got mad; he says I jump in and want everything clarified before he's finished explaining. We both started yelling at each other. We calmed down quickly and carried on with the discussion. Jack suggested that we need to treat each other with more respect. I don't quite know what he means, but I just agreed to keep the peace. We say good morning and good night to each other, but we sleep in separate rooms. I attempt to prepare breakfast and dinner every day, but it's a huge effort. I know my standards have dropped, but I'm not fit to do everything now. I signed the documents Jack wanted, in case he got angry again. Afterward, I gave him a kiss on the cheek and thanked him for taking the time to look after our finances so well. I'm a burden to Jack now… I know that, but it won't be for much longer.

Later last night, as we were preparing for bed, Jack asked me to look at his elbow, which was red and swollen; it looked like a tennis ball was attached. He called our doctor who asked him to come in tomorrow afternoon. Before we went to bed, Jack was shouting at me, telling me I was hopeless, that I showed no concern for him, and that the laundry has been neglected to the point where he has nothing to wear. I shouted back that he was bad tempered and asked him not to raise his voice. This morning, I offered to make breakfast for him, but he told me not to bother; he said he hadn't slept a wink and would get something to eat at the office. As he was getting ready to leave for the office, my heart was sore at the hostility between us. I tried to make small talk, but he wouldn't even look at me.

To get his attention, I said to him, "I keep dreaming about Jessica. It's not a good dream." He looked at me strangely and asked for details. When I told him about the murky pond with Jessica drowning and stretching out her arms to me, he looked at me intently. "Anything else?" he asked. "Yes," I said, "I try to move my arms to help her, but my arms don't move." His eyes dropped to the floor. "You're just dreaming about yourself. The MS. You have trouble moving. That's all. Put it out of your mind." Somehow those words rankled. *Out of your mind!* Is that what he thinks? Does he think I'm losing control of my mind as well as my body? Maybe it's my fault. Perhaps I should have accepted multiple sclerosis with a better attitude. Perhaps I should be determined to fight, but I don't see how I can fight the future. I have no future!

Kendra 35

It wasn't until six o'clock this morning that I picked up an assignment as a kindergarten teacher in Falls Church! I hurried to get breakfast organized and the children ready for school. Last night, I chopped up five mangos, so I could easily make mango smoothies for breakfast. With a sigh of relief, I dropped the children off to school, looking forward to a fairly easy day. Midmorning, we had a talk from the school bus driver, who told the children all about the safety rules and that he works fourteen hours a day. In the afternoon, the kids were working on making animal masks from paper plates. I could hear the word *Paris* coming from one table. I went closer and couldn't believe my ears. "When I grow up, I'm going to bomb the Eiffel Tower," were the words coming out of this little boy's mouth. I looked at the boy in astonishment and said to him, "That is the most wicked thing I've ever heard." He looked at me with a secretive little smile that seemed to say, "I know it's wicked, but I'm going to do it anyway." That boy is five years old. I feel very disturbed by that chilling scene. The only place he can hear this kind of thing is at home. I left the matter in the hands of the school principal.

I'm still glowing from my day at Harpers Ferry with Jack! I drove there with the kids, and we met for lunch. Jack came prepared with a picnic! He said there wasn't a decent place to eat. We found a grassy spot and settled down. While I was unloading Jack's car, he took my car to the gas station and filled up the tank for me. He really is thoughtful and generous. Jack's idea of a picnic was rather basic—sandwiches, sodas, potato chips, and cupcakes. We talked for hours. Jack confided that his daughter, Jessica, is pregnant. It's an awful situation! She had a relationship with an older man that ended. Very soon after, she had another short-lived romance. The problem is she can't identify the father! Jack is very worried.

In normal circumstances, Jessica would have confided in her mother, but Jack feels Grace is not emotionally strong enough to handle the situation now that she has MS. He feels that Jessica needs to talk to a mature woman rather than girls of her own age; her friends are encouraging Jessica to have an abortion, which is certainly one option, but Jack wants Jessica to consider other ways of dealing with the problem. "I wonder if you could talk to her, Kendra," he said. As if I don't have enough on my plate! "Well, if you think it can help," I found myself saying. I don't know if Jack means for Jessica to call me, but I would prefer not to get involved in this situation. During those few hours at Harpers Ferry, I was able to forget my problems while we picnicked in the sun. Now I seem to have taken on even more responsibility!

Grace 36

My "episode" is over, so I'm trying to get back to a more normal life today. I should have been meeting some friends for lunch at Congressional Country Club in Bethesda, but we woke up to several inches of snow. It didn't make sense for any of us to take unnecessary risks, so we reluctantly cancelled and stayed at home. My confidence was shattered yesterday by skidding on ice, so it's sensible not to venture outside. I haven't told Jack yet; the wheel alignment of my car is wrecked, and the bill will be thousands of dollars. It's hard to believe that temperatures over the last few days have reached over seventy degrees and now the mercury is below freezing. Our Virginia climate can be volatile. It must be affecting Jack because he's becoming volatile too.

I spent the morning moping around the house. However, the sun shone brilliantly in the early afternoon, and the snow melted easily, so I took the chance and drove to the grocery store. I'm trying really hard to keep the peace with Jack. This morning, as he was leaving for work, he looked out of the window at the snow-covered deck and wondered what coat to wear; the only possible choice was his heavy wool coat, but he decided to wear his raincoat. I couldn't believe it, but I couldn't stay quiet. I told him he needed to wear the wool coat, as well as a hat. He sighed heavily and put on the raincoat. I really wonder if he goes against me just to cause friction.

Take his will, for example. It makes absolutely no sense for those useless nephews to inherit anything. He's had very little contact with these people for decades. They don't care about Jack or about me.

Jack and I used to have so much in common. I suggested we might go away for the weekend, together, now that I'm feeling better, but he wasn't enthusiastic. Anyway, it's a bit of a nightmare traveling with Jack: he gets into a bad mood the moment we leave the house; the cab driver always annoys him; the check in process at the airport irritates him; and the security process really winds him up. Also, he gets mad when I give him any advice. It's just so depressing; he simply clams up and stops speaking to me. Even once we're seated on the aircraft, he refuses to have a conversation and sticks his nose in a business magazine. There's just no companionship anymore.

What's even more depressing is that Jack came home with a brochure for me to look at. A brochure on a short stay respite care home! So that's the kind of short breaks Jack has in mind—to get me out of his life. After twenty-five years of marriage to Jack, I'm an unwanted burden. I'm starting to think of ways I can release Jack from his burden.

Kendra 36

It's just so hard to get work! *The phone kept* ringing last night with horrible jobs in rotten locations. Who wants to get in their car and drive forty-five minutes for three hours work? I'm desperate for money, but that makes no sense. Just before ten o'clock at night, I bagged a speech and drama assignment at a middle school in Falls Church. What a relief! It was a demanding day—not intellectually, but it sapped my energy. The lesson plan was for the students to learn to project their voice, so the venue was the gymnasium, but there was a double booking. Groups of teachers were holding meetings there all day. I had to use the drama room to convince students to throw their voices in the confines of that small area; not difficult for them, but not easy for me to deal with their discontent. I had to do lots of improvising, by getting them to think up scenarios to demonstrate their imagination and acting skills.

I've not been smiling much lately. Jack made contact to offer me two tickets to the Washington ballet's performance of *Rock and Roll*. I was busy with the kids and told him I would call back. I'm reluctant to refuse his invitation. If I turn down his invitation, that will be the end of the relationship. If I accept the invitation, that gives encouragement for the relationship to develop further. I was quite happy the way things were. Jack is a best friend to anyone who is loyal to him. I want to keep him as a good friend, but I know that by turning down his invitation, the friendship will be over.

Really, I don't know what's got into Jack. I thought he was happily married to Grace. I wonder what it's like to be married to Jack. I imagined him coming home from the office at night. A kiss and a hug. Grace asks him about his day. He puts away his coat and his briefcase. He changes out of his suit into casual clothing. Sometimes he brings flowers…stopping at an upscale florist on the way home…nothing from a gas station. Dinner in their elegant dining room…maybe they don't use that every day. Perhaps dinner in the kitchen…a vast place with granite surfaces and gleaming stainless steel. A simple dinner…very healthy…but expensive ingredients. A glass of wine over dinner. Relaxing with coffee later in the evening. Not a care in the world. Money is no problem. The future is no problem. On special occasions… an anniversary or a birthday, there would be a fabulous gift; something from a designer store, something I could never afford, perhaps a handbag—something utterly adorable. The next day a shopping trip to buy designer shoes to match the handbag. Quite a contrast to my canvass tote and comfortable flip-flops!

Grace 37

My big consolation in all of this is Miriam; she checks, every day, to make sure I'm all right and encourages me to do as much walking as possible. We arranged to walk along the canal into Georgetown for lunch and walk back again today. I wasn't sure about such a long walk, but Miriam says we can come back in a cab if I'm exhausted. As I walked out of the house to get into the waiting SUV packed with chattering women, the excitement in the car was at high pitch as we set off along Georgetown Pike toward Canal Road. Our walk wasn't too exerting; after all, it's a flat towpath. We rewarded ourselves with lunch at Clyde's. Everyone was revealing their latest secrets: Joanna, how she screamed at her son; Petra, whose husband paid a fortune for an anniversary ring; Caroline, who is soon to be mother of the bride; Jean, who has just returned from a trip to Europe; Marjorie, who has been dealing with a burst pipe in her bedroom. It was just so good to get out, forget about the snow we've endured for the past few weeks, and put my "episode" behind me.

Jack came home with a gift: a glass vase filled with yellow roses. Did nobody tell him that yellow flowers are for friendship? The roses were withered around the edges. Rather ironic...maybe an image of what our marriage has become...a withered friendship. I can only assume he went to the store at the last minute and there was nothing else left, but it was a nice, spontaneous gesture. I wasn't sure what the flowers were all about, but, apparently, it's to brighten up the house when Jessica comes to visit on the weekend. Jessica didn't sound too well when she called yesterday; she sounds worried about something. I've got an uneasy feeling about Jessica, dreams of her in the muddy pond...something is troubling her, I'm sure. I've been disheartened by Jessica's response to my diagnosis. I thought she would be more caring. I suppose she is caring because she seems to think about all the practical problems I might encounter; she asked if I might want to move to a smaller house, without stairs; she's been making enquiries about a wheelchair, ready for my next "episode." Well, I've got my own ideas. There's not going to be another episode!

How to disappear? That's my dilemma. Right now, I'm picturing a car crash. Driving off a cliff could look like an accident.

Kendra 37

Today was an assignment at what's becoming one of my favorite schools! The class teachers are doing a lot of testing, and it seems that I've become a reliable resource. My students were grade two, so I was expecting a few problems— that's the age when they become a little overconfident. The class teacher was out in the hallway doing testing, so troubleshooting was a few steps away. What I didn't bargain for was the butterflies. The school is breeding monarch butterflies in the classroom. The classroom has a giant netted area filled with milkweed plants and monarch butterflies in various stages of evolution. Today, we had two caterpillars ready to shed their skin and become a pupa. We also had one chrysalis attached to some twigs, ready to become a butterfly. Anybody's guess when that would happen. Well, lo and behold, right when I was teaching grammar, a butterfly emerged! The children became totally hysterical, shrieking and yelling and disturbing the whole school. It was just impossible to contain the hysteria. The noise was deafening. Suddenly, I had an idea. I told the children that when they were born, everyone around them stayed quiet so they could get used to being in the world—they would have to do the same for the butterfly. A hushed silence immediately prevailed!

We had indoor recess today, during which time I allowed the kids to build a huge edifice with pillars and plates. It reached eight feet high, and we were putting the top plate on while the kids were chanting with excitement. Suddenly, the teacher from next door came in to find out what was going on. It didn't look good that I was encouraging the children to create all this noise. I later apologized to the teacher next door for all the noise during the day, but she was nonplussed. Her response was that the more disruption we have in life, the better. So it doesn't seem like I'm in the dog house, although it didn't feel like I passed with flying colors today.

This evening, after quickly changing my clothes at school, I arranged to meet Jack at a parking lot in Fairfax so that we could make the journey together to the Kennedy Center, along Route 50. Jack kept the radio on so that we didn't feel awkward. The news was all about the unrest in the Middle East, which gave us something to talk about on the journey. The guy at the box office recommended the restaurant on the corner, Rosa Mexicana, across the street from the Verizon Center. The atmosphere was perfect, casual and noisy, with gracious service. Dinner was the best part of the evening.

The performance of *Rock and Roll* was outstanding for choreography, but repetitive music, dull costumes, a lackluster storyline, and no scenery did not appeal to me. Some members of the audience left the theater before the end of the show. The atmosphere in the theater was one of dissatisfaction and disappointment. Somehow, the atmosphere in the theater matched my mood. We drove back to the parking lot in Fairfax with classical music playing in the car. I just wanted to go home and sleep. We wished each other a polite good night. We're both unhappy and seem to be gravitating toward each other for solace. I think it's best if I cut Jack out of my life.

Grace 38

It's been a tough week for Jack. On Monday, he left home at five in the morning, flew to Boston to meet some clients, stayed at the Marriott overnight, took the first flight to New York in the morning, attended several meetings there, then back to DC, all within thirty-eight hours; he was pretty exhausted when he got home, but I made sure to give him a good welcome. He says he's worried about the business situation; he needs talent to grow the company, but it's very difficult to attract the right caliber of staff into a new venture.

Jack was in a bad mood on Saturday morning. Jessica arrived, really early, in a cab from the airport, so we were wakened at seven o'clock by her ringing the doorbell. Normally Jack would make a point of spending time with Jessica, but he spent the day working out at the gym and watching a movie on television. Jessica was very subdued… I don't know whether something is on her mind or if Jack's attitude upset her. In the afternoon, she took herself off to the mall but came home without buying anything…most unlike Jessica. I usually cook Jessica's favorite dishes whenever she visits, but yesterday one side of my face became numb, which scared me. I had shooting pains in my legs, so I suggested we go out for dinner; we went to Dante's in Great Falls, the only Italian restaurant in the area that Jack will patronize.

On Sunday, we were invited to Uncle Bob's golden wedding anniversary party at the Officers' Club in Fort Myer. I just don't know what got into Jack on Sunday! Well, I do really. He has no patience for anything and gets riled up very quickly. We were behind schedule because we forgot about daylight savings this weekend. I had no time to do my hair properly, so was not in best form. We followed the directions to Wright Gate on Jackson Avenue only to find the gate was closed. Some passerby advised us to go to Hatfield Gate, but we couldn't find it. Jack was driving around like a maniac, screeching round corners and braking suddenly at junctions. I was holding on to the door handle to keep my balance. Then he started yelling at me that I've become hysterical. I never even opened my mouth! I yelled back at him that he needed to control his temper and treat me with respect. So we stopped communicating. Eventually, we found the place and got into the fort, after a further delay of having the car searched by security.

The champagne buffet brunch was most enjoyable, so Jack calmed down and relaxed. The other guests were charming but quite ancient, mostly in their eighties; Jack said he felt like he had just graduated from college. I did enjoy the company of the elderly people; they all have much in the way of life experience. At one point, I asked Jack to remind me of the name of a street where we used to live. I guess it's a long time since I've seen him in a social setting. My heart flipped as I wondered where my Jack has gone.

Jessica wasn't invited. I suppose they didn't expect her to be in town, so she amused herself catching up with some old school friends. She admired the beige brocade suit I was wearing; she also admired the new shoes I bought to complete the look—two extravagant pairs to choose from; one pair of Prada and one pair of Louboutin. Jessica rarely admires anything I wear, so I gave the shoes to her thinking it would cheer her up. I know she loved the shoes, but it didn't seem to brighten her spirits. I wore more sensible shoes to the event; it was silly of me to buy those shoes. I could easily trip over and make a complete fool of myself. Maybe Jessica can wear the shoes to my funeral!

Kendra 38

It's been quite a week so far! I've spent hours and hours on the phone trying to get work. I've been successful, eventually, but I'm sure I spend more time trying to find work than I do actually working. The children are getting neglected, so I'm feeling guilty about not giving them the attention they deserve.

Yesterday, I worked at an elementary school in Reston. I've never been there before. I always thought it was too far away. I'm getting increasingly desperate, so I'll take anything now, no matter how far I have to travel. Mapquest advised the journey would take fifteen minutes, so I allowed forty-five minutes to cope with traffic. What traffic? It was all going in the other direction toward Tyson's Corner, along Leesburg Pike, so I zoomed along with no difficulty and lots of time to spare. On arrival, the class teacher was there, trying to put together lesson plans. She was wearing her pajamas and looking in bad shape. I tried to steer clear of her breath, as she was exuding germs. Thankfully, there was enough time for me to interrogate her since she had everything scrawled in barely legible handwriting. As she left, I looked around the room in horror. It seemed like a tornado had hit the place. Everywhere I looked, there was chaos. My biggest concern during the day was the germs in the classroom. I've never seen so many sick children. Thankfully, it was a small class of only nineteen children because ten were absent, but all I could hear was coughing and sneezing. I asked those who were sick to raise their hands. Eight little arms shot in the air. Half the class was sick. I gave them all a lecture about washing their hands and not putting their hands anywhere near their faces. Immediately, all hands came down and the children were conscious all day long about hygiene. I could feel the germs attacking me all day. It started on my throat and worked its way into my chest.

Now, I'm spreading these germs to my own children. It's unavoidable, but I'm doing my best. I won't allow them to give me a kiss or a cuddle. Hopefully, I can overcome the infection and not spread it to everyone around me!

Jack's not solving any of my problems. The only contact from him has been a brief message on my Blackberry the day after we went to the ballet together. I haven't replied. Stanley isn't solving any of my problems either. I'm running out of money, and the kids all need new shoes. I did ask Stanley if he could stump up the money for the shoes, but I'm still waiting. Su is still waiting for the new car he promised her, too. Stanley seems to be attending a lot of sports events, so I guess that's his priority rather than his family!

Grace 39

We were expecting Jessica to visit for the weekend, but she called off an hour before she was due to arrive by sending a text message to Jack; she knew I would have blown my top if she called, so she took the easy way out. I was so angry. In fact, I was white-hot angry! After the anger wore off, I wanted to cry. I went upstairs and did just that; the disappointment was hard to bear. These young people just don't know how you yearn to see them; they don't realize how their presence enlivens your world and gives meaning to your existence. But, after all, there is no meaning to my existence!

Today is Easter basket day. It was really hard to pull out of the event. My basement is now clear of all the parcels of colored grass, plastic eggs, little soft bunny toys, plastic pails, and much more besides. The other ladies will have to buy all the candy. Gathering all that stuff together and then wrapping and tying each gift with ribbon would be too much for me. It all looks so appealing, a huge treat at such low cost for underprivileged families in the area, but I just couldn't bear the thought of twenty women coming to my house to make all this happen. I think there will be about two hundred gifts, so it will be hard work. Standing in the same spot, doing repetitive work is sore on my hands and puts a strain on my back; I'm just not fit for that kind of physical work anymore. It certainly makes me sympathetic to those unfortunate women who have to do repetitive manual work every day.

Miriam has taken everything into her basement, and the ladies will work from there; she's such a wonderful friend and neighbor. I don't know what I would do without her. When it's all over, there will be a little bit of fun. I ordered sandwiches from Subway in Great Falls, so once the baskets are stuffed, everyone will stuff themselves with sandwiches, chips, sodas, and any leftover candy. If I can make myself look presentable, I should show my face at lunch, but I don't think I'll bother. I'll need to persuade one of the ladies to take on the responsibility for next year; perhaps I'll make the excuse that I'll be traveling.

I've been investigating Dignitas, the assisted suicide organization. I always wondered how it all worked and why you hear about people in Europe departing the world this way, but not in the United States. I learned that I can cease to exist by drinking a cocktail of fruit-flavored drugs, or use the cheaper option of inhaling helium gas. The whole operation is regulated by lawyers and physicians. I discovered that Dignitas only operates in Switzerland, and their fees are more than some people earn in a year, so that course of action is not practical.

I also investigated assisted suicide here in the United States. I discovered that, legally, I can end my own life in the state of Oregon, but I would have to be resident there for six months, so that course of action is not going to work. I don't think assisted suicide is the way for me to go. I wouldn't be able to do it without Jack knowing. A car crash would be much easier.

Kendra 39

I was up at five o'clock again this morning trying to find work! I was lucky on the second attempt. It only took twenty minutes. The start time was eight-thirty at one of my favorite elementary schools in Vienna. The assigned subject was art, so I was in heaven, so relaxed and smiling while making breakfast for the children. It would be much easier for me to let the kids have lunch at school, but I can't afford the cost. I can do boxed lunches for a week at the same price. A whole bunch of bananas is really cheap. With a few granola bars and a bottle of water, I can give the kids a healthy lunch at very low cost.

I love teaching art. Today, all the classes were assigned to create greeting cards. The instruction was to think about designs, shapes, lettering, medium, message, and colors. My final class was working well. As usual, I toured the room to check on progress. I discovered that one boy had not folded his card as instructed and had written, "I declare war," right across the inside. I asked him what kind of card it was supposed to be, but he could provide no answer. Giving him instructions to draw a design on the front, he drew two crossed swords on the page. I expressed my concerns to the boy's grade teacher. She shrugged, stating that he's just a goofball. She says she often has to censure his essays because they're not suitable for a boy of his age: nine years old. As I was leaving the school, I decided to alert the school counselor about my concerns. She was so appreciative of the information. She told me this kind of thing often goes unreported when it's obvious there's stuff going on in a child's world that is mirrored in their creative work.

Before I got home, I had to go the post office, since some of my mail is going missing. I also had to follow up on returned items that I had purchased online from Macy's. I sent the packages by USPS insured delivery, but the suppliers have no record of receiving them. Why is everything so difficult?

I haven't heard anything more from Jack. Well, I didn't return his call, did I? I suppose I was hoping he would call me again. I do want to call him now, but I'm not sure what to say. Do I tell him I'm looking for work? Do I say I'm getting desperate for money? Do I tell him the kids need new shoes, but I can't afford to buy them? Or do I tell him I think he's the most wonderful man I ever met and I wish he was mine?

Grace 40

Jack was moaning that I hadn't collected his shirts from the laundry, so he made a trip to Nordstrom on the weekend. Not only did he buy ten new shirts, he also bought three pairs of designer shoes. He spent several thousand dollars, but he tells me he needs to look good this week. I would like to look good too, but no amount of designer clothing will improve my appearance now. I just don't care anymore. I'm dragging one foot, my voice is weak, my hair is a mess, my nails are dreadful, but it just doesn't matter. I spend most of my time in my dressing gown, clutching Bruno to my chest… I'm just like a child with my teddy bear… Bruno's soft, cuddly presence is my only comfort some days. So what to do with the rest of the day? Edward dropped by on the weekend and gave me a present of a Kindle; he says it will be much lighter than a book for me to hold in my hands. Such a thoughtful boy; he was hoping to see Jack, but he was out at Nordstrom. Edward hasn't talked again about his lifestyle; I'll leave it for him to tell Jack in his own time. This afternoon, I tried using the Kindle; I bought my first book, a thriller based on a true-life story. I spent the afternoon curled up on the sofa, with Bruno beside me, reading a book...or reading a Kindle, I should say.

I couldn't decide what to make for supper. Jack has been in meetings for the past few days, where all the meals are provided, so he's not hungry when he gets home. I decided to give him a special treat. I made scones and invited him to a tea party, using his grandmother's famous china. The china is so beautiful with twenty-four-carat gold design, a real family heirloom. I also used the silver tea service that belonged to my mother's family. I have cherished all these items, but no one will want them when I'm gone. I mentioned this to Jack; he says I need to make a note in my will about who should inherit all the antiques in the house. Maybe he has a premonition that I'll be out of his life soon; that will take a lot of the stress out of his life! As soon as the scones were finished, Jack poured himself some vodka. I gave him the evil eye because he's drinking too much, but it didn't stop him pouring a few more during the evening. I think my attempt at trying to make a cozy evening together made Jack feel uncomfortable; he only seems comfortable at home when he's occupied—either on his cell phone or packing for his next trip. I don't pack Jack's case anymore. Sometimes I even wonder if there's another woman in his life.

My head feels full of pressure and both legs feel weak. I wasn't sure how I would cope with the lunch arrangement on my calendar, but my friend from Chicago won't be in town after all—disappointing but also a relief. I had a whole day ahead of me, with nothing planned, so I forced myself to get washed and dressed and made my way to the Galleria this morning. I've been invited to attend an accessory exchange next week, but I've got nothing suitable to donate. So I bought a designer silk scarf at Saks. Hah! After I'm gone, they'll all remember me! It's really silly and extravagant, I know, but I just can't throw any old thing into these exchanges; people will talk. I don't want to have a bad reputation after I've gone. I want everyone to say, "Remember the time when Grace donated a brand-new designer scarf?"

Kendra 40

I was so looking forward to today! I got the job by phoning direct to a school in Reston, where I have a good relationship with the administrator. She fixed me up with a grade three class for today. The start time was eight-thirty, so the thought of a nice, long sleep filled me with relief, but I was wide awake at four-thirty in the morning! I don't feel too bad now, although there's something going on. I think I've got a temperature. Maybe I picked up something at one of the schools. Looking on the bright side, the children's lunchboxes are better whenever I'm losing sleep.

I'm always early for work. There are always problems to solve—a classroom door locked, lesson plans missing, or technology that won't work. Today, the special education teacher came to introduce herself and told me she would co-teach because so many children in the class have issues. Fairfax County has a high percentage of children with learning disabilities because the funding is good. Parents actually move here so their child has access to all the testing and resources. In my class of twenty-four, there were so many children with special needs that an instructional assistant had also been assigned! I certainly could not have coped alone with that bunch; herding cats would be easier! I've been haunted by one boy, whose behavior was very alarming, all caused by emotional disturbance. He's the cutest-looking ten-year-old boy you can imagine, but there were times when he was behaving like an animal, crawling on the ground, making grunting noises, and trying to bite other children. I've learned that he has been in foster care three times with a view to adoption, but each time he has been rejected because his behavior is too difficult. I was content to simply have him not wrecking the classroom until we spent time working on art. The assignment was to draw a picture of a fictional world. This boy produced an amazing galaxy of planets and chattered lucidly about all the details. I haven't stopped thinking about this little boy. What does the future hold for him? Apparently, his current potential adoption is unlikely to proceed. This time, the foster mother might be unsuitable since she's started to display erratic behavior.

I came home thinking that if I was still with Stanley, I would suggest that we might be able to give shelter to that little boy. However, under my current circumstances, I'm barely able to offer shelter to my own children. Where is it all going to end? I'm feeling so weary now!

I called Jack. I couldn't hold out any longer. Thinking about that little boy at school made me think how easily money could alleviate the child's problems. I poured out my concerns to Jack, babbling on about my day. He shared some of his business problems with me. He says I understand the business situation better than Grace. Jack ended the call by saying, "Stay in touch."

Grace 41

I had quite a fight with Jack last night. He came home earlier than expected and was annoyed that the house was in disarray. He was, also, angry because I had forgotten to collect his shirts from the laundry. He was shouting at me really loudly. I snapped back with a few insults but quickly set about preparing a meal. After dinner, which we ate in silence, I realized the laundry didn't close until seven o'clock, so I got in the car and came back with his shirts. It was quite an effort, but I'm not leaving this world with him thinking bad things about me.

I just don't need any more stress in my life—it brings on my symptoms. I think I've got another "episode" brewing. My feet are burning, my legs are tingling, there's an odd feeling on my face that travels from below my eye down to my collar bone, my forehead is numb, and my breathing is shallow. When I was shouting at Jack, I could feel my tongue was numb.

I was invited to Miriam's birthday party today. Although I was feeling dreadful, Miriam persuaded me to come because I could walk there and back. I did manage to shuffle there, slowly, without falling over. All the guests were asked to bring a gently used accessory to exchange rather than bringing gifts; that meant loads of beautifully wrapped packages, we could all have fun, but Miriam would not end up with a bunch of unwanted gifts. My eyes feasted on all the gorgeous wrapping, huge boxes with pretty bows, tiny packages promising big surprises, and handsome totes with lots of color. I started dreaming they were gifts for Jessica's wedding. It would be nice to have something to live for, but then I imagined myself as mother of the bride—an embarrassment. So what was I going to contribute to this accessory exchange? After all, I do want to be remembered fondly once I'm gone. Each gift is supposed to be a secret, but you know that everyone's eagle eyes are watching to see which package belongs to you. My contribution was the Dourney & Burke bag that Jack gave to me as a gift several years ago; it's too heavy for me to carry now, so I don't use it anymore. Jessica would probably like it, but there's plenty coming her way. Anyway, she'll probably enjoy the Chanel sunglasses, which were my choice in the exchange. I'll give them to her next time she's here. I've no idea when she might visit again; she calls Jack instead of me these days.

We went to Wildfire for dinner last night, on the spur of the moment. We didn't talk much. Jack mentioned Jessica several times without telling me anything; he seems to talk to her about business now and cuts me out. When we got back out into the parking lot, Jack commented that I should apply for a disabled badge to make parking easier. As he reversed, another car came into view behind him, and the driver started blaring his horn. Jack immediately threw open the door, ran to the window of the other car, and gave the driver a piece of his mind, shouting and yelling and cursing. The other driver could so easily have had a gun. Thankfully, the other driver drove away. Presumably, he wanted our spot but not a confrontation. Jack would never normally behave like that. He calmed down once we got home, but this anger is something new. It scares me.

Kendra 41

Today I was at an elementary school in McLean. What a great school! I'm so impressed by the dedication of the teachers and the diligence of the students. My students were shy and polite at first but gained confidence in me by the afternoon. One little girl had been claiming my attention all day. She just couldn't sit in her seat. She constantly came to my desk to give me advice about how things are usually done, as well as reminding me of the time and begging to do all the high-profile jobs such as being line leader or handing out worksheets. At the end of the day, she was at my side again to ask if I could come back tomorrow. Somehow, she started telling me about her home life. She has never met her father. Her parents had a fight, she tells me. Her father was treating her mother like a slave until, one day, she told him to iron his own shirts, and then he walked out. It's not the full story, one assumes, but a simple story for the little girl to understand. She is such a lovely girl. I would love to speak to her mother to compliment her on such a lively and happy child. That's one of the many downsides of substitute teaching. I won't get that opportunity.

Since I have a full week's work ahead of me, I thought about treating myself to a haircut at Eclips Salon in McLean. However, after tax, it will take a full day's wages to pay for my haircut. I really have to do something about my financial situation, but I'm working so hard just to find assignments each day, never mind the time spent in the classroom that I've made absolutely no progress. Reading a fairy story to the kids today, I realized that's what I need. I need a handsome prince to solve all my problems!

I called Jack. He did ask me to stay in touch. It quite surprised me how energized I felt on hearing his voice. I chatted all about my day. He told me his temporary assistant is driving him wild. I was hoping he would ask me to come and work for him, but there wasn't even a hint of that. I wonder if he wants me to ask for the job. We agreed to meet once he returns from San Francisco.

Grace 42

I detest winter. It's cold, dark, gloomy, and so depressing. Now I see skunk cabbage appearing in culverts, and the dogwood and redbuds are in blossom. It should lift my spirits, but it doesn't. The only thing that lifts my spirits is junk food and cuddling Bruno. I haven't been sleeping well. The soles of my feet are burning, and I have pins and needles in my legs. My neck and throat are painful. I can ignore the pain during the day, but not at night. I can't go on like this much longer. I know another "episode" is coming.

I escaped from my symptoms for a few hours on Saturday evening. We had a long-standing arrangement with some friends to see *Shear Madness* at the Kennedy Center; it's the longest-running play in the history of American theater. It was just what I needed…some lighthearted comic relief that leaves you feeling all your cares and troubles are much less serious. My heavy heart certainly soaked up all the farcical action on stage. Dinner at the Terrace Restaurant before the show was quite good. Everyone was very attentive to me, including Jack; he can put on a very good show in public. Jack spent the interval gazing at posters for upcoming events and was late returning to his seat. We all gave him questioning looks, but he passed along packets of chocolate raisins, giving the excuse of a long line at the counter. Jack never buys candy at the theater, and he knows I wouldn't eat chocolate raisins; he does do things that are out of character these days.

Miriam dragged me to a fashion show in Chevy Chase yesterday. I don't have any interest in fashion anymore, but she persuaded me that all I had to do was sit quietly and enjoy a nice lunch. Sitting quietly and eating is about all I'm good for now. I've given up walking with Miriam and her friends; it's just not possible to keep up with them anymore. Hah! My next new gown will be a shroud! I wonder how I'll look in a shroud.

I so wished that Jessica was with me; just seeing those ladies having fun might just let her think of having a different life… of a married woman with children rather than her career-girl lifestyle. A dear friend seated next to me tried to persuade me to get involved in a gala she is planning for September. I put her off by saying I was hoping to be on a cruise around that time and couldn't take on the responsibility. It's not totally a lie. I've decided I want to be cremated and have my ashes scattered on the Potomac River, so I do really plan to do some cruising, but not quite what my friend envisaged.

This afternoon, I looked for a place to crash the car. I found myself driving around Chesterbrook and turned off onto a road within a new development. I found a fairly good spot… I could easily imagine driving off there! The houses are under construction, so I could simply go through one of the driveways and over the cliff. It would seem like I was checking out the house and lost control of the car. When I looked at the spot in detail, I realized there were some flaws—it's not really deep enough, and there's lots of dense trees and vegetation. It looks more like a pond for run-off water. I would probably survive if I drove off there… I would need a lot of speed to be able to hit the bottom of this shallow ravine with great impact; that wouldn't be possible because I would have to drive uphill to the house on a twisting bend, which would slow me down, then I would have to turn into the driveway and put my foot down hard on the gas pedal. I think I would just nosedive into the ravine and get stuck in the undergrowth. I would probably only sustain injuries, and I would cause distress to the owners of nearby properties. This is not the spot. I need to search again.

Kendra 42

Today I snagged an assignment to teach business education at a high school in Reston. Arriving my usual fifteen minutes early, it seemed strange that nobody was in the office. Guess what? I was at the wrong school! Arriving ten minutes late, I raced along corridors to find a classroom full of teenagers and an anxious teacher holding the fort. The lesson plan was three lines of instructions: to keep classes working on their current projects on Photoshop and creating basic visual programs. I hoped I would be teaching marketing or creating a business plan or some other interesting project. Basically, I was babysitting and spent the time confiscating cell phones and iPods! Of course, I knew that every time my back was turned, they were switching to computer games. Several boys gained permission to leave the room—one to go to the clinic and two others to go to the bathroom. After they were out of the room, I realized they had all been seated together and left large backpacks behind. Just think how easy it would be to bring explosives into school, excuse yourself, and then leave the building! I can get a little paranoid, so I tormented myself with an internal struggle not to overreact, but they were gone a very long time. Thankfully, they returned by the end of the period, probably having spent the time smoking in the bathroom. Really, these kids are so plausible to your face and then take every liberty. I was so relieved to have survived the day, which was an early finish, so I knew just how to celebrate. I drove to the nearest Subway, got myself a sandwich and a coffee, and then sauntered into the nearest salon for a manicure and a pedicure. I know that was self-indulgent, but I needed some pampering today!

The last two days have been quite a contrast. When I came home from yesterday's assignment, I wouldn't exactly say I was exhausted. I think I was just slightly traumatized. My assignment was teaching third grade at an elementary school in Falls Church. The lesson plan was five pages long, so I knew I was in for a tough day. The children arrived all cute and shy, but some were quite obviously from underprivileged situations. When one little boy took off his sweater, I noticed he was covered in sores, so I sent him to the clinic. An administrator called into the classroom to say the boy was covered in bites from bed bugs and was running a fever. Just what we all need!

I came home feeling unclean and threw every stitch of my clothing into the washing machine! What am I doing? I should have stayed in my nice, comfortable job as an executive assistant. I've been such a fool! How can I get out of this mess? The only solution is Jack! I called him for consolation. I knew he would sympathize. I found myself blubbing like a baby. Jack calmed me down with soothing words, telling me I did the right thing quitting Leo's job. "Everything will work out in the end," he assured me. Somehow, Jack makes everything feel better. He has that gift. I saw it, every day, in the office. "One last thing," he said. "I wonder if you would talk to Jessica. She'll be here next weekend. Can you meet with her and talk things over?"

Grace 43

I found the place; it's perfect. Jack wanted to drive through Shenandoah National Park on Sunday, so I agreed to a comfortable car journey. I invited Miriam and Bob to come along; having company in the car would be a good excuse to escape the tension in our household. Sunday was a fabulous day—a bright blue sky, not a breath of wind, the countryside dazzling. We set off around ten o'clock, heading for the north gate at Front Royal, and took the hundred-mile trip on Skyline Drive, along the crest of the Blue Ridge Mountains all the way down to Rockfish Gap. By noon, we had reached the Skyland restaurant, at an elevation of over a thousand feet, and were quite hungry. The dining room was pleasant with expansive views of the wilderness. The temperature had reached seventy degrees, but we decided to have lunch indoors; we skipped the buffet, which seemed to be geared to the taste buds of little children, but enjoyed club sandwiches, along with several cups of strong coffee. By two o'clock, we judged we were not even halfway through the park, so we turned back, took the Thornton Gap exit, driving home via Sperryville and all the other little towns on the way toward the Beltway. Shortly after leaving Skyland, Jack wanted to admire the view from Hemlock Springs Overlook; he stopped the car, and we wandered around the rocks. I was very intent on watching my foothold and looking out for snakes. I brought along a walking cane, which Edward gave me as a little gift; he's the most thoughtful one in the family; he thought it would help me keep my balance. Without it, I wouldn't have been able to admire this view. I suddenly realized this was the spot...there's no barrier there... I can drive the car straight off the cliff and plunge into an abyss below. It's very, very deep...miles and miles of rock, so the car would keep bumping off the rocks and gain speed on the way down. The car would probably burst into flames well before it hit the bottom of the ravine. At the bottom, it would maybe set a few trees alight but would be unlikely to cause a forest fire. Nobody else would be hurt, and no property would be damaged. It would look like an accident. The only difficulty is my family wouldn't be able to understand why I had driven all this way alone without any explanation and without telling anyone. Maybe the police would classify my death as an accident, but my family would suspect the truth. Well, it doesn't matter; I can't think of everything, and I can't think about how my family will feel. They'll be shocked at first, I expect, but they'll be relieved when they realize that I'm not a burden to them anymore. So I've chosen the spot, and now I need to choose the time.

Kendra 43

As a thank you for agreeing to spend time with Jessica, Jack gave me two tickets to *Le Corsaire*. He put the invitation across in a businesslike fashion, and I accepted in similar tone. He picked me up from the apartment this time. We talked about Jessica all the way along Route 66. When we reached the Kennedy Center, we grabbed coffee and made our way to comfortable arm chairs in the Hall of Nations. Sitting casually together wouldn't raise alarm bells if we are spotted by an acquaintance, I thought.

I poured out all my woes to Jack. I was so mad at Stanley. He promised to bring a new car for Su on the weekend. He told me all about it, a blue Chevy—he had it all detailed, he would tie balloons to the mirrors, and he would deliver it at two o'clock on Saturday. Three hours later, after constantly trying his cell phone, I got hold of him. He told me it didn't work out. I completely lost the plot. I was yelling and screaming at him, down the phone. It took the whole weekend for me to calm down. I was so angry! Su didn't get mad. She just became a lump of misery. Her father has no idea what he's done to her. In the past, he's always let us down as a family. This time he let Su down personally. She'll never forget that. I was still angry about it, when I was telling Jack. He listened patiently, and then a comfortable silence developed between us while he allowed me to simmer down. I stared into the distance at the sunset over the Potomac. Jack put his hand over mine. "Don't worry," he said, "I'll fix Su up with a car."

My emotions were running wild! I was feeling sorry for Jessica, miserable for Su, angry with Stanley, and I didn't know what I was feeling for Jack. The ballet performance was magnificent, but I couldn't stop thinking about Jack all the time. I was so conscious that he was sitting next to me. Eventually we were both gasping with amazement at the genius of the performers, and the audience roared with approval at the end of the evening.

We didn't talk much in the car on the way home. Jack played classical music on his radio, which maintained the hot-blooded mood of *Le Corsaire*. When we reached the apartment at the end of the evening, Jack turned off the car engine. My nerves were jangling. I didn't know what to do. I turned to look at Jack. I was looking at my best friend. "Come back and work for me," he said. These were the words I had been longing to hear, but it wasn't enough. I didn't answer but got out of the car. Jack accompanied me to the apartment. Once the door was open, I couldn't close it again!

Grace 44

This weather is so volatile, a thirty-degree difference between one day and the next, which seems to match Jack's mood swings. But I don't pay much attention to Jack anymore. Jack is focused on business. I have my own business to deal with.

I attended a fashion show yesterday at Neiman Marcus in Chevy Chase…yet another one of my charities trying to raise funds. I decided to go along to say secret farewells to the group. Driving along Wisconsin Avenue, my symptoms became acute—burning sensation on the soles of my feet, tingling in my legs, numbness in my throat, burning on my tongue, tenderness on my skull, swelling on my gums, my neck felt strangled, and my breathing was shallow.

I should have stayed at home really. I was a danger on the road, and the day was a disappointment. Over a hundred women are members of this group, but only fifteen turned up to the event; too many chairs and too few attendees didn't create a good atmosphere. The store did a fabulous job providing champagne and canapés while the models showed off the most exquisite gowns. A total stranger latched on to me, saying she was on the store's mailing list and received an invitation to the event; she provided the sideshow for the afternoon by scooping canapés into a bag when she thought nobody was looking while trying to ingratiate herself with animated conversation; she also seemed to be circling the handbags that were left unattended. The others felt sorry for her, saying she probably hadn't eaten in weeks, but all I saw was a thief. Eventually, she realized I was closely observing her, so she scurried away, but not before stealing another load of canapés. The show finished earlier than expected, so I wandered through the store on my way back to the car. A cosmetic assistant inveigled me into purchasing some merchandise. My makeup needs to look good on my last day on this earth, so I spent an hour and several hundred dollars preparing to look my best on the day of my departure from this world.

When I got home, I felt dead…emotionally dead. All I can think about is the car crash. I'm not sure whether I should write a suicide note.

Dear Jack, Jessica, and Edward,

Forgive me for taking what, I know, may seem like a coward's way out.

I can't help you with the business problems anymore, Jack.

You don't need me, Jessica. You have a wonderful career ahead of you.

You have a lifestyle that suits you, Edward. May you always be happy.

Please know that I love all of you. You are my flesh and blood.

My body is failing me, and I am failing each one of you.

I have become a burden to everyone around me.

We all need a purpose in life.

I believe my purpose now is to end my life.

By taking this action, I hope you see that I am giving you a gift.
My departure from this life gives you the gift of freedom.
May each day bring you joy.

With all my love,
Grace

Kendra 44

I got to school today and realized I forgot to wear my watch and my lipstick. Jack is on my mind all the time! In the past, the children have always been on my mind. Every second of the day, I was thinking about the children and what they were doing. Jack has taken over! No matter what I'm doing, I'm thinking about Jack, and the children have faded into the background.

I didn't look good at all today, nor did I feel too well. I had bagged a great assignment at an elementary school in Falls Church but wasn't sure how to get there. I checked the directions just before going to bed. The activity got my brain very lively, so I couldn't sleep. I was teaching first grade, a really lovely bunch of kids. The only apparent problem was one little girl. Thankfully, the lesson plan highlighted the difficulties. Immediately, the child entered the room, I made friends with her, and she was good as gold all day. She's a really bright child and solved the math problems quicker than anyone else, but she can get distressed very easily; the child was quite charming, so I'm sure she'll work out fine as the years progress. Suddenly, there was a boy standing in front of me with a bright-red face and tears running down his cheeks; he swallowed something. I rushed him down to the clinic; he stopped breathing on the way. The emergency services were called, and so were his parents. The object he had swallowed was the end piece from his glasses. It turns out he has done this before. Quite a drama, but he survived!

Right now, I'm feeling drained emotionally and physically! I've been doing all the chores while checking the system for assignments, and I can't stop thinking about Jack. I feel lonely at the thought of not having Jack in my life! I wonder how he feels.

The children have gotten used to my evening routine of looking for assignments while I make dinner. They do their homework while this telephone ritual takes place. They seem able to switch off and concentrate without any difficulty. However, I think today has to be my last in this routine. I'll have to give some responsibility to Su. I'll have to make her responsible for making breakfast for everyone. She can also make up everyone's lunch boxes. I think she's old enough to understand that I need her to help me.

I wish Jack was here! The kids really like him. He could help with their homework. What a difference his guidance would make to their grades at school. There's been no further mention of me going to work for Jack. I'm afraid to broach the subject. I'm afraid to break the spell. I'm afraid of saying or doing the wrong thing. I'm afraid of losing him.

Grace 45

Jack came home last night, and all I heard was business, business, business! On the phone the whole time! Talking to this one, talking to that one! In between phone calls, all I heard was mutters and moans about business issues. What I want doesn't matter! He never asks me what I want! He just gives me what he thinks I need. He tells me what he wants to do, and I have to work around what he wants. Well, not this time! This time, I'm calling the shots! I'm taking control. I've written another suicide note.

I'm angry!

Angry! Angry! Angry!

I have no control over my life!

Why have I been given this curse?

I don't deserve this!

I've been a good wife.

I've been a good mother.

Now, I can't be a good wife!

Now, I can't be a good mother!

My feelings don't matter anymore.

My feelings have never mattered.

My life has been yours.

Now, my life is slipping away from me.

I've devoted my life to you,

To my husband,

To my son and my daughter.

Now, you don't need me in your lives.

Well, now my feelings do matter!

I want to do it my way!

When I'm gone, you can think about this.

Jack, you need to think of someone other than yourself.

Jessica, you need to seek happiness beyond your boundaries.

Edward, my thoughtful boy, you need to divulge your secret.

Forget about me now. It's over!

Finally, I get what I want.

I've gone to another place.

A place of my choice!

Jack better watch how he treats me now. If he continues to treat me like a thorn in his side, I'll be leaving today's note for him!

Kendra 45

Jack says Grace is out of control! *She was* screaming at him last night and using foul language. He asked Jessica to come and visit over the weekend since that seems to improve Grace's moods. I'm meeting Jessica for coffee on Saturday morning to help discuss her problem. She has to choose whether or not to keep this baby, but since she doesn't know who the father is, this is an added dimension to the problem. Thankfully, she has plenty of time to make her choice. Under normal circumstances, she would be able to decide whether the father should know, but she can't do that since she can't identify the father. Right now her choice is simple: keep the baby or have an abortion. I can't tell her what to do. As a mother, I can only tell her it's not an easy life bringing up children, even when there is a father around. This decision will affect the rest of her life. She may, later, meet the right man, but if she aborts, she'll never forget this child and will always have regrets. If a new man comes into her life and she has kept the baby, he will need to love her enough to take on the responsibility of another man's child, conceived in irresponsible circumstances. Of course, she can have the baby and decide later if she wants to divulge the truth and suggest DNA testing before deciding on adoption. I can't tell her what to do. All I can do is lay out the possible options. She has to make her own decision. I suppose I should feel honored that Jack is using me as a surrogate mother to Jessica, but somehow it feels like I could be blamed for whatever decision she makes. Jack won't say what he hopes for Jessica. He doesn't say anything more about going to work for him…or about a car for Su.

So, with a lot on my mind, I wasn't looking forward to today. In desperation, I accepted an assignment for kindergarten at a school where the behavior and hygiene of the students leaves a lot to be desired. What was I thinking? But I was pleasantly surprised. The instructional assistant was delightful, and the classroom was bright, clean, and well organized. However, my misgivings returned when the instructional assistant told me that after twenty years in the same classroom of this school, she plans to resign. The disrespect from students, even at this early age, is so low that she can't continue. She blames the recession and the stress that families are enduring. In my opinion, unsupervised TV viewing is another big factor. The whole family unit is suffering, she said, and it's reflected in classroom behavior. Early in the day, I used the bell to call students to order because of the incessant talking. One boy yelled out that I was not to do that again because it was really loud and very annoying. I told him quietly that I would ring the bell as loudly and as often as I liked. He seemed quite shocked, but his behavior was fine afterward. Indeed, he seemed to respect me after that, and we were developing a good rapport. However, he later drew a stick figure with a bubble coming out of the mouth that said, "I hate you." I was amazed he could spell that, but he wouldn't tell me who this referred to.

At the end of the day, I spoke to the guidance counselor who told me the boy is regularly aggressive with other students and the person he hates is himself. This boy is crafty, aggressive, and destructive. It's actually quite scary. What will he be like as an adult? Anyway, I can't start worrying about this kid. I have my own family to worry about—and my meeting with Jessica!

Grace 46

The dreams never go away; sometimes they come during the day...sometimes, without sleep...Jessica in the muddy pond...but now she has her back turned; her arms are reaching, but she can't see me... I can't help her. New dreams now...dreams of the car crash. I wake up in terror. Jack would have to identify my body! I can feel my face crushed by the metal. If I can feel this, it means I'm still alive... I survived...my plan has backfired. A disfigured cripple is not the solution. I need a fatal car crash. My only comfort is Bruno... I clutch my teddy bear to me...he's a very big boy...his arms wrap around me... he's warm and loving...he's always there...he never lets go...he doesn't talk...he just listens...he understands...my tears dampen his fur...he shares my grief...he wants to come with me on my journey... I don't want to hurt Bruno. I've started to think of another plan...a better plan...yes...a much better plan... Jack will come home and find me. That will shock him! An overdose would be so easy and painless. Jack will come home and find me...looking beautiful...but gone. I have my suicide notes... written in my best handwriting...on my best notepaper. Jack will find me... I'll be clutching an envelope...he'll take it from my hand and read…and he'll be sorry…so, so sorry…but…maybe when he pulls the letter from my hand…maybe it will be difficult to take the letter from my hand… I'll leave the letter on the table beside me… I'll be wearing my best gown…maybe an evening gown…yes…full makeup…most glamorous gown…and Bruno in my arms… I like it…yes, that's what I'll do. I need to say good-bye…I need to see my loved ones, for the last time. I need to see Jessica and Edward and all my friends. I want to gaze on their faces. I want to look my best. I want to leave behind good memories. Everything has to be planned. I need to deal with all the practical issues. I want the house to look perfect when Jack finds me. I need to get that new housekeeper geared up. I need to consider my last wishes…make sure that's in order. I'll have to be buried somewhere… I need to leave instructions for my funeral. I think I want a private service…just Jack and Jessica and Edward…don't think it's appropriate to have eulogies and all that nonsense…not under the circumstances. Can't bear the thought of everyone whispering. I've already chosen the music… Sarah Brightman singing, "Time to Say Good-Bye." As the curtains close on my coffin…as the fire consumes my remains… those glorious soaring notes will accompany me on my journey. I want my ashes scattered on the Potomac…maybe in Great Falls Park… I wonder what music would be appropriate… I'll ask Miriam what she thinks about music for the park…no…can't talk to Miriam…no music in the park…just the thundering roar of rushing water…washing everything away…all my fears…all my pain…washed away. I'm so looking forward to all of this… I'll be in control!

Kendra 46

I arranged to meet Jessica at Brio's in Tyson's Mall. She's a very attractive girl—tall, slim, long dark hair. I suppose Grace would look like that when she was young. It felt very odd to be acting as a counselor to this young woman. I'm amazed she agreed to talk to me. But that's just Jack! It's hard to say no to him. When I saw her, I gave her a hug and a kiss. It seemed appropriate. After all, we were about to embark on a very intimate discussion. She's a nice young woman with a serious disposition. Any man would be proud to have her as his wife. She's attractive in such a natural way—no makeup, hair sleek and shiny.

I started our chat by commenting on the restaurant; then we spent time discussing the menu. I wanted to wait until lunch arrived before broaching the subject. "So, Jessica, you find yourself in difficult circumstances," I offered as a way to introduce the topic. She smiled and flushed. "I can only tell you the difficulties of being a single mother," I continued. She listened while I outlined my own marriage to Stanley.

Once she was ready, I started to ask some questions. The poor girl is utterly confused. There's no way she wants to marry the second guy, so that makes things a little simpler. She's desperately in love with the first guy, but they broke up because he wasn't ready to settle down. He's now aware that she's pregnant but wants her to have an abortion. He says if the child was his, things would be different. It's obvious this guy doesn't love Jessica. He's telling her to kill what might be his own child.

But I didn't state my view. I didn't state any of my views. I don't know how to advise her. It's not my place to give her advice. We just spent time doing what she must have done already with her friends—considered all the options. I put myself in Grace's shoes. What advice would Grace give her daughter? I don't think Grace could bring herself to condone the abortion of her own grandchild. I really think it's a mistake not to tell Grace. I know she's unwell, but knowing about this isn't going to kill her. She'll be distressed and emotionally disturbed. Knowing about the situation may bring on an "episode," but what mother wouldn't give her right arm to help her daughter in these circumstances?

I'm sure Grace would advise Jessica to have the baby and decide on the next course of action once the child is born. Every instinct in me wanted to say, "Tell your mother," but Jack has already made that decision. He doesn't want to upset Grace. I can see that he wants to protect Grace, but I think she has a right to know. So that gives me a dilemma. How do I report back to Jack? I want to tell him that Grace should be informed. But if I say what I think, how will that affect my relationship with Jack? I finished my talk with Jessica by saying, "Well, young lady, you have a lot to think about, but you have time on your side. If you're seriously considering abortion, you should contact one of the clinics, but whatever you do will leave you with regrets. If you have an abortion, you will have some regrets. If you have the child and give it away, you'll have regrets, too. The only way you won't have emotional damage is if you keep the child, but that will change your future. You'll be giving yourself a difficult life. Only you can decide."

I think Jessica found it helpful to talk—not just to me but to anyone who might listen without passing judgment. It's not my place to judge. I just hope Su never gets herself into a mess like this. I'll need to have another talk with her about the potential pitfalls ahead of her. Actually, I think Su is more mature than Jessica when it comes to this kind of stuff. Su is more wordly, really. Jessica may be a high-powered career girl, but I think she has a more vulnerable personality. Su is more streetwise, I think, even though she's still at high school. Teenage girls, today, seem to know it all. She probably knows more than me. Oh dear, best not to think along these lines. My next problem is what to tell Jack. I'll just say it was good to meet Jessica, I think it was helpful to talk, and she needs to talk to more people. I've done what he asked!

Grace 47

I have nothing to live for anymore. The final blow has struck! Jack told me that Jessica is pregnant and is planning an abortion. He said he thought it was fair to tell me now so that I could talk to her if I wanted. He says she talked to a lot of people, including Kendra. Kendra! Is he out of his mind? What has Kendra got to do with our family? She was his secretary, nothing more. She has no rights into our private life. And my daughter talked to this woman—a woman she has never met before because Jack told her she could trust her advice since she's been living as a single parent. He doesn't tell my daughter to come and talk to me because he thinks it will make me unwell! How that man's mind works is beyond me at times.

I'll call Jessica and give her a piece of my mind. How can she cut her mother out of this problem in her life? Her father's advice, that's what—that's what stopped her talking to me. If she was going to keep the baby, maybe I would have something to live for. I could look after the baby. I know I'm not fit to do anything strenuous, but the baby could be here and I could do some things. Jessica could come and live here, have the baby here, go back to work when she's ready; employers cope with these things nowadays. This is my grandchild! I don't care who the father is; this child will be my own flesh and blood, and Jessica is considering ending its life! Well, if this child dies, I'm going to die along with it. I'm going to call Jessica tonight and give her a piece of my mind.

I suppose everyone else is telling her it's her own decision. Well, it's not her own decision! She's going to kill my grandchild! If she lets this baby die, I'm going to make her feel really guilty. Oh, yes! Another suicide note is on the way.

Dear Jessica,

You're my daughter and I love you,

but I don't know you anymore.

You talk to strangers rather than me.

You won't talk to your own mother.

You killed my grandchild.

I can't forgive you for that.

I know that child.

I dream about that child.

That child is in a muddy pond,

reaching out to me.

I want to be with my grandchild.

You all have each other.

That child is alone and defenseless.

Nobody loves that child.

Nobody wants that child.

Nobody loves me.

Nobody wants me.

Well, I want my grandchild!

I'm going to the same place.

Marel Brady

I need to help my grandchild.
That baby needs love.
I'm going to find that baby.

Kendra 47

I felt quite despondent after talking to Jessica on the weekend, so I was really looking forward to a day at school to forget about that situation. When I arrived, the team teacher greeted me on arrival to tell me I might have a difficult day because the sub from yesterday wouldn't come back. I like a challenge, so I was tough on the kids in the first five minutes. They soon got the message. Language arts went fine, and I got through math without showing my deficiencies. Next on the agenda was science. There were no instructions and no materials. I hope never to encounter that again. I called for help from another fifth-grade teacher, who was horrified that I was expected to cover that assignment under those circumstances. She suggested that I ditch the assignment and tackle something else. But what else? If you have twenty-eight eleven-year-olds who are not stimulated, you're in for a rough ride. So while showing a video about creatures of the ocean, I figured it all out. Thankfully, with the help of two special education teachers who dropped by, we actually completed the assignment successfully. The ingredients were sand, sugar, salt, and water. I could just imagine the potential chaos. But I made the kids work in teams, appointed team leaders, and made them responsible for leading the experiment and ensuring the classroom stayed in good shape. The students responded brilliantly. At the end of the experiment, two students offered to clean all the containers and put them back in their boxes. They did a terrific job, gaining a special mention on my report. At the end of the day, I told the students they were a fantastic class, and we did high-fives all round.

I drove home with lots on my mind. As I made myself a cup of coffee, the phone rang. I could see it was Jack calling! I wondered whether to answer. I just wanted to savor a wonderful day rather than talk all about Jessica. We talked for quite a while. Jack is having a rough time with the business, and Jessica has decided to go through with the abortion. I listened carefully and gave him some sympathy. At the end of the call, I was surprised to receive a proposal from Jack. He wants me to take a temporary assignment with him as his executive assistant on a week-long trip to Los Angeles and Phoenix. My thoughts were whirling! I was thinking I do need the money, but a week with Jack could be a catalyst for trouble. I'm in love with a married man. I don't know if he's in love with me or if I'm just a better companion than his ailing wife and an escape from his troubled daughter. I'll have to think about this very carefully! I was hesitant and told Jack I would let him know my decision by tomorrow. He followed up by saying, quite casually, "Oh, by the way, that car I promised for Su will be delivered on the weekend." I was stunned. Jack has kept his promises! He's providing work for me and a car for Su! Stanley never kept his promises!

Grace 48

The past few weeks have been surreal... I don't know myself anymore. How could I have done such a thing! I'm stupid and cowardly, that's how! If I had taken all the pills at once, it might have worked...taking them gradually had a different affect on me. I started taking them at ten o'clock in the evening. I knew Jessica or Edward wouldn't call at that time of night, and they would be too busy getting to work in the morning to think about calling me. Jack was due home from a trip to the West Coast in the morning. My plan was that Jack would find me, dead on the sofa, with all three of my suicide notes beside me. So I took four painkillers; then half an hour later I took another four pills; then half an hour later, I took six more. Nothing happened! I just had a weird buzzing sensation in my ears... I didn't even fall asleep. Two hours later, I took more pills. I drifted off with a satisfied image of myself. I was wearing the pink ball gown from the last event I attended with Jack... the one where he danced with all the other ladies. My hair was looking good, and my makeup was perfect. I wore shoes I couldn't possibly walk in anymore—black evening shoes with little straps, diamante all over, and huge high heels. I hid my plain slippers under the sofa. I held Bruno by the hand... I didn't clutch him to my chest because I wouldn't need him anymore... Bruno could go to a new home. Someone else will need Bruno just as much as me... I was thinking of Jessica's baby...the baby Jessica doesn't want would love Bruno.

Jessica, Jessica, Jessica. How could you do this? You're not my daughter anymore. I thought about how life would turn out for my family in the future, a future without me. A few years from now, Jack would have another woman in his life. Jessica would be a misery, drinking too much, gained a lot of weight, and stopped caring about her appearance. Edward would be happier; his secret would be out, no longer hiding his lifestyle. My plan had some effect. I woke with Jack shouting and yelling, "Oh, my God! My God, what has she done! Stupid woman! How could she do this! Dear God, why have you given me this! I can't deal with this! Take it away! Take it away! I'll have to call an ambulance! Who do I call? The police? The ambulance?" I watched Jack as he paced up and down, yelling with his hands over his face. My heart felt like stone. I wanted Bruno to comfort me, but he was gone. My farewell letters and envelopes were scattered on the floor, taking up space on the polished wooden surface, like stepping stones in a river. I stayed motionless, watching Jack's every move and listening to him yelling. I didn't feel good, my head bursting, my body still. I couldn't move, although my legs and arms felt as if they were quivering. I didn't want the police or an ambulance, so I tried to make a noise. Jack stopped yelling, ran over and stood, staring at me. He just stared and stared. He didn't say anything.

Kendra 48

I accepted Jack's proposal! I joined him, as his assistant, on his trip to the West Coast. He's still employing a temp from an agency who's looking after matters in the Tyson's office. What a difference to my life being back on board with Jack! Lots of clients to meet and meetings to attend. Our first stop was in Los Angeles, based at the Marriott Hotel in Torrance—not luxurious, but the location really suited the purpose, equidistant from a number of clients. Jack took me with him everywhere: to a dinner at Kincaid's on Redondo Pier, to a lunch at the Terranea Resort in Palos Verdes, and, on the following day, to an informal breakfast meeting at the Kettle on Manhattan Beach, to a lunch and conference at the Trump Golf Complex, and to dinner with some long-term clients at their private home in Rolling Hills Estates.

It was so easy to be with Jack! I found myself holding his hand as we walked along Manhattan Beach early each morning. The next stop was Phoenix. The weather was fabulous, in the nineties every day, with no humidity. Our base was the Camelback Inn, an excellent choice since most of our meetings were in the Scottsdale area. Our time was more relaxed, so Jack managed a few games of golf at McCormick Ranch with some clients while I spent time shopping at Fashion Square. We dined at some of Jack's favorite places: Cowboy Ciao in downtown Scottsdale, Kona Grill at the mall, the Hermosa Inn along Lincoln Boulevard, and the White Chocolate Grill in Kierland. Our last evening was magical. We were guests of clients who own a fabulous property up at Desert Mountain. The surroundings are amazing. It's easy to be smitten by the atmosphere. I succumbed to the intoxicating feeling of being in a different world. All my longing to be with Jack was satisfied.

Quite naturally, we held hands as we wandered in the grounds of the Camelback Inn at the end of the evening. We didn't need to speak. Jack pulled my hand in the direction of his casita. We gently undressed each other and made love…deep, mature, satisfying, bonding, sensual, and exquisite. The next morning, over breakfast, there was no embarrassment, just a natural feeling of togetherness.

Should I have taken the assignment as Jack's assistant? I have no regrets. Working alongside him again was like coming home. Being with Jack feels like just the right place to be…our souls seem to have merged together. Last night was truly magical—haunting flute music in the gardens as we strolled back to the casita…the desert air caressing our skin…the stars twinkling in a clear sky…the perfume of jasmine and gardenia floating in the air. When Jack touched my hair…his kiss was commanding, demanding, full of longing… I couldn't resist.

I don't care about anyone else now. I don't care about Grace and all her health issues! I'm not Jessica's mother—she can solve her own problems! All I care about is Jack!

Grace 49

I'm taking antidepressants now along with medication for MS. I'm feeling very calm as I think back over my actions. I want to get back some kind of connection with Jack, but we look at each other in bewilderment. There's no connection… just like looking at the face of someone from the past who comes to visit occasionally. At least my actions had some value. Jessica planned to visit the abortion clinic the day after my "bid for freedom," as she calls it. When Jack called her that morning, she came straight here and hasn't left my side. She got such a terrible shock. I feel ashamed that I put Jessica through that kind of situation when she had her own worries. I shouldn't have yelled at her when I found out about the baby. She still has time to go through with the abortion, but she tells me she's having second thoughts. I think she's going to keep the baby! I think I've made her see that a baby is a gift, not a choice. I think she sees she could take time off at home with me here. We could employ a nanny who would keep an eye on me too. If we get a properly qualified nanny, that would be a lot better than some untrained foreigner in the house.

Jessica drove me to Fairfax for a doctor's appointment this afternoon. Afterwards, she suggested having coffee at the Café Amour in Vienna. As we looked at the array of delicacies in the glass cases, someone tapped me on the shoulder, an acquaintance from one of my charities; she asked about Jack and then mentioned she had seen him recently at a ballet performance in the Kennedy Center. I responded that Jack hadn't mentioned seeing her. A heavy silence followed, and I sensed that something was wrong. Was she trying to tell me something? My mind started racing. How odd for Jack to attend a ballet performance—he has no interest in dance. I tried to imagine Jack in the audience and couldn't make the picture fit together. This must have been a business invitation, but then I began to wonder why the invitation hadn't been extended to me. There's no reason why I can't sit through a performance at the theater; maybe he just hasn't been letting me know about these things anymore. All kinds of other questions started to gather in my head but never quite formed themselves into a sentence.

A headache started at the base of my skull as I wondered whether to ask Jack about his visit to the Kennedy Center. Jessica was tugging on my sleeve. "Mom, what kind of cupcake would you like?" We didn't stay long at the coffee shop. The hospital visit and the drugs were taking their toll on me. When we got home, there was Bruno on the sofa, giving us a welcome.

Kendra 49

My first paycheck from Spelectra came through today! Jack has been very generous, although I can't understand why I haven't heard from him. He has arranged with the human resources people for me to be listed as an independent contractor so he can use me on a consultancy basis. He still keeps the temporary assistant from the agency in the Tyson's office. She doesn't want to travel, so he can take me along instead. This arrangement lets me carry on teaching, and the flexibility of being a substitute means I'm free to join Jack whenever he needs me. I'm not sure how good this arrangement will be in the long term, but it's a boost to my life in every way at the moment. Also, thanks to Jack, Su is driving around like queen of the road with the car he provided. It's way too good for a teenager, so she's taken on quite a little swagger on those hips. With Tamara by her side, she looks very grown-up as she does her baby-sitting act. Tamara and Tiramisu! My two favorite sweet things on the planet!

The clocks changed last weekend, so we have more daylight, and everyone is smiling as the sun chases winter away. I'm going to chase away the winter blues by spending some money. The children will get those new shoes they need, and I think we need a family treat…perhaps a visit to the movies at the weekend. And I'm going to spoil myself. That haircut at Eclips is on my list of things to do. I might even treat myself at their spa. I've never been there. Oh, how wonderful a life of luxury must be! No money worries and looking good every day would certainly float my boat!

I wonder how Jessica is doing. I was tempted to give her my phone number when we met but decided against leaving myself open to further involvement. That poor girl must be going through torment! At least I never had that kind of issue to deal with. I may have been a teenager when I married Stanley, but there were no added complications. What a fool I was to marry that guy. I should have waited until I was more mature. Maybe then I would have married a man like Jack.

I can't understand why Jack hasn't called me. Does he regret everything? How does he feel about me? I'm in love with Jack—he must know that! I don't think he can allow himself to fall in love with me! Grace is the problem!

Grace 50

Jessica returned to Boston, having extracted two promises from me…I agreed to stop taking the antidepressants and to start getting involved in all my activities again. "After all, Mom," she said, "I've taken your advice. Now you have to take mine." I agreed to the bargain. Jessica totally disagrees with taking antidepressants. "They just mask problems, Mom, and you'll have no emotions," she declared. I'm not sure how she comes to this conclusion, but I'll go along with her wishes. I'm just so overjoyed that my grandchild is safe! I'm thrilled at the thought of a new life in our family. I know it won't be easy for Jessica, but I'll give her as much support as possible.

Edward has been fantastic. After the drama of my actions, Edward's secret was no big deal, but it's done nothing to foster good relations with his father. Jessica stayed for only two days, but it was the best two days I've spent in several years. Just having everything out in the open has made such a difference. We were able to talk honestly with each other. In the past, I hardly knew what Jessica was doing from one day to the next. Now I know so many of the details of her daily life. My actions have brought about quality time with my daughter, which has been sadly missing. The situation made Jessica become my little girl again; she was able to confide in her mother; she needed her mother. I was useful again, not just the weakling in the litter. I just wonder if my escape attempt had been successful, the baby may not have survived. I'm looking on my actions as a catalyst for saving the baby's life—I really believe that.

I think my letters got to Jack. I don't think he's forgiven me; maybe he'll never forgive me. I'm not sure I care really; he can carry on spending his time on Spelectra. I don't even care if he moves out... I would probably be happier without Jack... I'm sure he would be happier without me.

Miriam doesn't know anything about all this; she's my best friend, but I don't have to tell her absolutely everything. Jack didn't call an ambulance; he decided I wasn't in danger of dying, so the neighbors are unaware of my actions. Maybe Jack was hoping I would die! Maybe that would suit him just fine! Well, I don't care. I've got a grandchild coming into the world. I'm going to welcome this child with open arms. Jack can do what he likes. I'm going to take Jessica's advice and get my life back in order. Top priority is deciding on any changes I want to make to my will. I realized these are things I should have done before even considering taking my own life...these matters need attention. I'm feeling hopeful that I have a useful and joyful future in front of me.

Kendra 50

Today, I was teaching kindergarten again!
Jack was on my mind the whole time! This morning was fine, until one little boy got very upset because he didn't win a game. He took off his glasses, threw them on the floor, and pummeled them with his little fists. I spoke softly to him and explained he was unlikely to win because it was a game of chance rather than skill. He's a very bright boy and completely understood the math of the situation. Then there was the cutest little girl who returned from PE shouting that she had the most terrible time of her whole life. She became almost incoherent, babbling away about the horrors of hoops and balls, and running and jumping. I guess she's not going to be a sports personality! Two other little girls were a disappointment today. Most unusual! It's normally the boys who are the problems. One innocent little thing actually used the F word. I had no alternative but to write a note home to her parents. The other disappointment was a little girl who refused to accompany another girl to the clinic. I explained that she needed to respect my authority and follow directions, so she reluctantly complied. Later, she apologized for her behavior. I accepted her apology, which was very genuine, but, again, I

carried out the regular teacher's instructions by writing a note home to the parents. She took the note with tears running down her face and shoulders heaving. She told me her parents would shout at her and make her miserable. I explained this was just a lesson to be learned. She needed to follow directions courteously. I told her to simply tell her parents that she apologized and that I forgave her. The tears dried up, and she went back to her desk with a contented smile on her face. I finished the day with tears in *my* eyes. I couldn't bear the thought of the parents shouting at this vulnerable little girl.

I had given up hope of hearing from the recruitment agencies, but when I got home, there was a message on the answering machine checking to see if I was available for a temp job in the summer. I suppose I could do it, although it's not what I'm after. I asked them to keep me listed.

By the time I sat down with a coffee, I was feeling unsettled. Jack hasn't been in contact for several days! I've heard nothing from him since our trip to the West Coast! I was startled to read an article about Spelectra. *The Post* has gotten wind of the troubles within the company. I'm torn—should I call him tonight? Does he need my support?

My life feels emptier without Jack! He must have regrets about our trip together. I know I'm chasing him now. I hoped he might have fallen in love with me, but he's in a different place from me. He's not free. I'm not really free either, I suppose. I'm still married to Stanley, but that can easily be changed. If Grace wasn't an invalid, things would be different for Jack!

Grace 51

This week has been a whirlwind. Before she left, Jessica went through my calendar and made me call and accept all the invitations I had ignored or declined. Between us, we generated such a positive attitude and a lot of energy. Jessica is smiling at the thought of her baby being welcomed into the family. I'm smiling because I have a reason for living. It was so, so good to spend time with my daughter... I've missed her so much... I'm hoping she might come back to live in Virginia.

So this week I've been to Green Spring Gardens in Alexandria, the Marco Polo Restaurant in Vienna, a gourmet lunch at a home in Chevy Chase, a fund-raising lunch at the Embassy of Cyprus, and an art exhibition in DC. I should be exhausted, but I'm not! My body seems to have bounced back from the shock treatment of all those pain killers! The doctor says I'm "in remission," so I should make the most of this time, without going overboard. He wants me to see a counselor or a therapist, but I told him I don't need that. I've got a grandchild arriving to chase my blues away!

The art exhibition was such a privilege. Miriam won the visit at a fundraising gala and asked me to come along as her guest. The art collection is owned by a lady who has built up a private collection over the years. This little lady is one smart cookie…a psychotherapist who owns a string of successful art galleries on the East Coast. The collection at her home got started on her first wedding anniversary when she asked her husband for artwork rather than jewelry to celebrate the occasion; she and her husband have never stopped collecting. Miriam and I were just thrilled at the latest pieces in her collection: a glass sculpture by Gilhouly, three ceramics by Picasso, four major paintings by DeLuppa, as well as many other truly amazing contemporary creations. Every piece of furniture is contemporary, and every available space is adorned with something truly fabulous. Today, the lady of the house graciously took us on a tour, showing us all the bedrooms, her husband's library as well as her own; even the art deco bathrooms were revealed for our enjoyment. It felt like inhabiting a little piece of heaven being enveloped in such beautiful surroundings.

I just wish I had the sense to collect art when I first got married. Artwork can be admired every day instead of having the items locked away in a safe, and it's a much better investment than jewelry. I must suggest to Jessica that she does that… I'll buy her a painting to celebrate the birth of the baby. I already told her that she'll fall heir to those paintings we bought in the Wentworth Gallery; she was thrilled because she's a great admirer of Ferjo.

I must say I was happy to be alive today. The sun was shining, and the whole world seemed to be smiling. Jack is the only person in my life who is not smiling!

Kendra 51

How could Grace do such a thing? She's such a selfish woman! She has no idea of the stress Jack has been under with all the business pressures! Jack said the doctor was more concerned about him than about Grace. After all, he's already had a heart attack. If she was trying to kill Jack, she's going about it in just the right way. The shock of finding her like that could have made him drop dead! I don't feel bad about being with Jack anymore! He sounded like he was in a trance when he called me. He apologized for not being in touch. Coming back from our romantic trip together to find Grace slumped on the sofa was an emotional roller coaster, he said. A romantic trip! He actually said that!

I was hoping Jack might have mentioned another work assignment, but I guess he has his hands full right now. I don't see why he can't get rid of that woman who looks after him at the Tyson's office. I could do that job; then I wouldn't have to be looking for work every day on the sub system, just like a day laborer.

However, today was another interesting experience in the world of teaching! I had one little boy in second grade who frequently took his shoes and socks off and scattered them around the classroom. Also, whenever we had to walk in line through the school, he insisted on being the line leader. He did walk in a straight line, but he was spinning around all the time. I tried this spinning action at home. It does give you all-around peripheral vision, but it quickly makes you dizzy! Another issue today was with two boys. At recess, one reported that the other told him he couldn't wait for him to die. These kids don't dream these things up. They must be hearing this at home! I held a conference with the two boys, accompanied by another boy who had witnessed the event. It seems the boy used this remark because he objected to being chased around the playground. I pointed out that his response was too severe, very hateful, and should never be used. The boy who had done the chasing explained he didn't mean any harm, and the other boy offered an apology. In the afternoon, it was the girls who were a handful. One little girl, who looks like a Barbie doll and behaves like a demon, was trying my patience with constant attention seeking and never-ending questions. She started her antics at recess by going missing when I blew my whistle to bring the class in line. Eventually, she was called to heel, but as we entered the building, she tried to escape again. I can only assume this little girl receives no discipline at home. Oh, and then there was the other little girl, always staring into space and not concentrating on her work. I then discovered she had a photograph of a pop star in her desk, inside a folder full of love notes. The handwriting was far superior to anything she used when writing about synonyms! In love with a pop star at seven years old! Oh, dear. What does the future hold for these little girls? But never mind that. What does the future hold for me? Anyway, at the end of the day, I came home feeling satisfied that my contribution to society was worthwhile.

I came home to an empty apartment. The children were all at after-school activities. Just that sound of silence was bliss. I made a cup of coffee and scoffed quite a few cookies while channel-hopping on TV. Next thing I know, I'm woken up by Su's backpack hitting the floor. I looked at the clock. I had been sleeping for an hour. I guess I needed a rest, but I should have been preparing dinner. My first thought was Jack. When am I going to see Jack again?

Grace 52

Yesterday was Easter Sunday. We spent the day as a family, with Jessica and Edward paying a flying visit. Jessica looked well, although a little tired. Edward looked terrific. It seems that someone has given him a makeover; he was wearing a navy blazer and white slacks, absolutely the latest fashion, Jessica confided to me. It looked more like a throwback to the roaring twenties, but his hair was all gelled up, so I guess that part of his image was trendy, and I did take time to compliment him. Jack was subdued all day. I guess he hasn't forgiven me…he probably never will.

I got the new housekeeper to prepare dinner for us before she left on Friday; she's quite helpful, really; we're getting used to each other. All I had to do was switch on the slow cooker and heat side dishes in the microwave. As we sat down to dinner, Jessica announced she had some news to reveal. My heart skipped a beat, but she was grinning from ear to ear, so my initial fear that she had changed her mind about keeping the baby vanished as she announced that she plans to study for an MBA right here in Virginia. She has several offers and just has to decide which one to accept. I dropped my fork as excitement flooded through me.

"So you're coming home, Jessica?" "Yes, Mom, the firm has given me twelve months leave of absence. I told my boss about the baby, and between us, we came up with this arrangement."

I broke down and cried. There I was sobbing my heart out at the dinner table on Easter Sunday.

Kendra 52

So Jessica is coming home! Nice for her and nice for Grace! Two casualties who can't do anything right. I didn't say anything when Jack told me. I could see he's troubled by the whole scene. He does acknowledge that Jessica will come out of this with a stronger career path in front of her, but what happens to the baby once she has her MBA? Who will look after the baby? Jack thinks she's just taking time out to have a lot of fun and then she'll dump the baby somewhere while she gets on with her life. Does she think that by staying at home with Grace she can get all the home comforts and then walk away? She's been up there in Boston, leading the single life, binge drinking and getting herself into a mess, and then she thinks she can come home, have all her problems solved, and then move on. She thinks she can loll around in luxury all day long, with the housekeeper doing all the chores, while she has a great time attending classes and writing essays. Some get it so easy in life! Jessica is granted leave of absence from a really good job to get an MBA while I can't afford to send my kids to college!

I had to get out of the apartment yesterday, so I took the kids to Alexandria as a weekend treat. Jack arranged for Su's car to be filled up with gas so we could enjoy an inexpensive day out. We're still in his thoughts, even though he can't be with us. He understands how difficult it is to survive on a low income. My family is in the ninety-nine-percent bracket in society while Jack is in the one-percent bracket. How I would love to wave a magic wand and be in the stratosphere of Jack's privileged world for the rest of my life! Anyway, Alexandria was so hot and humid that we didn't stay long. The temperature was in the mid nineties. The day before was sixty degrees, so it was difficult to adjust to such a sudden hike in the mercury. We wandered in and out of antique shops with me telling the kids, "Don't touch," every five seconds. Jack gave Su a hundred dollars so we could have lunch at RT's. He knows I love Cajun food. I wish Jack could have been with us, but he had reports to read, and I guess it would have been too much of a public place, too near home; he could have bumped into someone he knew. If only we weren't in a clandestine relationship! It would be such a joy to have another day out with Jack and the children, like the day we spent at Harpers Ferry.

After lunch, we snooped around an art exhibition at the Old Torpedo Factory. The kids loved being able to run around there, without the "don't touch" instructions. They also loved sitting on benches at the waterfront, watching the world go by. I savored Jack's last phone call to me. He asked me to make arrangements for some clients to attend a concert at the Verizon Center. This is a great opportunity for me. I'll get a nice fat check from Spelectra, and I'll get to see Jack! He says I can come along without raising any eyebrows. Also I'll get to meet more clients. Networking seems like the only way I'm going to get a decent job offer. I'm going to be quite brazen. I'm going to look my very best and make sure the conversation is all about me.

Grace 53

Jessica and Edward were here at the weekend…a surprise visit. Sunday was Mother's Day. I wasn't expecting much; young people are so distracted with their own lives. So I glumly sat down to an early morning cup of coffee. I was looking my most unattractive, hair all over the place, shabby robe, no makeup, barefoot, and sporting a disgruntled expression. The doorbell rang. I expected it would be one of the neighbors; they've been away on a trip, and I've been collecting their mail and newspapers. I wasn't fit to be seen, so I asked Jack to answer the door. I heard voices calling out, "Happy Mother's Day," but it wasn't until the footsteps echoed on the wood flooring that I realized it was Jessica and Edward. Jessica had flown out of Boston in the early hours of the morning, and Edward had picked her up at the airport. There they were, laughing and full of fun. Jessica needs to take better care of herself; she can't go flying around like this anymore, but this was not the right time for scolding. "Come on, Mom. We're taking you out of here," Jessica cajoled.

I needed to have a shower before I could think of anything else, so we both climbed the stairs together, arm in arm, returning an hour later, looking fresh and smartly dressed. "I noticed a Mother's Day service advertized at that quaint church on Lewinsville Road as I drove past," announced Jessica. "You know, that Middle Eastern church. It's some kind of Catholic place, Melkite or something. Let's go there and have Sunday brunch afterward." I don't know what's got into that girl. She wanted to go to church the last time she was here. Reluctantly, I agreed to the plan, but only after hearing that Edward had made a reservation at River Bend. I didn't know he kept his membership there after he moved. Jack stayed at home; he said he would meet us at the restaurant.

As we entered the church, the priest was conducting a baptism, and the first words I heard were, "Death is an insult in the face of God." I felt like a thunderbolt had hit me. I could hardly concentrate on anything after that. We sat down on pews at the back of the church. I should have been paying attention. There was some big deal going on…a deacon being ordained or something. I just couldn't think straight with all that sensory overload, incense and chanting, and processions of men in colorful embroidered robes. The words of the priest kept going around in my head. Afterward, in the restaurant, I felt as if I was disembodied. I was chatting with my family, but those words kept going round in my head. I almost felt as if I was drugged… that feeling when you're about to go into surgery and you're not totally in this world. As I put my head on the pillow last night, so many thoughts swirled in my mind; the deacon's words kept echoing in my ears. My attempt at death seems so intertwined with the birth of this baby! I don't know what it all means. It seems like there's some kind of karma involved. I suppose I've been resurrected from the dead and the birth of Jessica's baby is a miracle I've been longing for! I don't know. It's hard to figure it all out. There's some kind of spiritual message here, but it's elusive.

Kendra 53

Jack dropped by for half an hour on Saturday. He was carrying a fabulous arrangement of flowers. I've never seen anything like it! The card attached was from Ultimate Florists in Great Falls, but Jack had not written any message on the card. He just said he wanted to pay homage to the best mother in the world. I was astonished "Me?" I questioned. "What about Grace?"

He just shook his head and frowned. "It's Mother's Day tomorrow," he said. "I think you deserve something nice." He chatted with the kids, asking what's going on in their lives, but he looked uncomfortable and preoccupied and didn't stay long. "When will I see you?" I asked as he was leaving. "The Verizon Center," was his answer.

So…it's nearing the end of school year. I was expecting my third-grade class to be a bit wild today because students seem to get overexcited toward the end of term. As I entered the building of my absolute favorite school, I realized there probably won't be many more teaching assignments in the few weeks ahead. So I decided to make the most of the day and give my absolute best to the students. As the children arrived, I greeted each one with a huge smile and asked them to find their name on the attendance list. I haven't used that approach before. I've always been too focused on studying the lesson plan as students arrive. One girl commented as she entered the classroom, "Oh, that's a good strategy." Well, my new approach seemed to cast a spell on these children. They were as good as gold all day. An hour before the final bell, while the children were busy writing an essay, I gave the class a compliment. I told the class that I was very impressed. I explained that I normally have several names in my report about students who displayed disappointing behavior, but, today, I did not need to mention any names. I told the class their behavior was fantastic today, and I hoped they could keep it up until dismissal time. The reactions were so amusing. One boy asked me several times if I was sure his name wasn't on the list for bad behavior. Eventually, he explained that he behaved badly most days. Another boy asked if there were any names on my list for good behavior. I replied that everyone was good. Perhaps one or two students had been a tiny bit disappointing, but not enough to mention on my report. Well, at the end of the day, I got two love notes. The first note was signed by three girls who wrote, *"Thank you for being a wonderful teacher! We really enjoyed you! Have a nice day! You're so nice!"* Underneath the message was a big heart with a smiling face. I was very touched by the note and gave the girls a group hug. The other note was from one boy who wrote, *"Thank you for this wonderful day. I wish you could stay for another day. Thank you for all the education. I hope you enjoy your letter and weekend."* Underneath was a big heart with a smiling face on either side. I gave the boy a big hug too. I was quite taken aback when another boy voiced a thank you, saying today had been awesome. I looked at him with surprise, and then another boy chimed in, saying today was really special. As the classroom emptied, I sat down at the desk with tears in my eyes and shook my head in astonishment. I honestly couldn't believe the feedback from these children. Maybe I'm quite good at this teaching stuff.

Perhaps I really should become a certified teacher. I wonder if I ought to figure out a way to get qualified!

Grace 54

I took the notion to get back with my painting group. For years, we've been producing artwork for auction at local charity events. We've raised a lot of money with unique wall panels, stenciled furniture, decorated mirrors, and similar original items. I made a bunch of phone calls and, hey presto, more than a dozen ladies were delighted to get together for some new projects. It's been too long! Last night, I prepared sketches on panels and drew some contemporary designs. Our theme will be flowers, so today all the ladies made a start on colorful contemporary panels. The camaraderie was so enjoyable that I actually found myself giggling... I can't remember the last time I laughed, never mind giggled. I felt like I was back in high school! I just wanted to be silly. That's one of the reasons why art is good; it's so therapeutic.

Last night when Jack came home, I mentioned that I received a voicemail from our credit card company. Jack went into panic mode, insisting that I follow up immediately. So I called the number and, after speaking to several agents, established they simply want to update our information. Somehow, after the call, Jack got all hot and bothered and started yelling at me. I yelled back, and we hurled a few insults at each other. I don't know what gets into him sometimes. Later he asked if I had calmed down. I didn't answer, and he went straight into the library and slammed the door. A few minutes later, I called that dinner was ready. I left his meal on the table, which he ate alone… I lost my appetite.

I tried to make the peace with Jack. Later in the evening, the library door was open, so I ventured to ask if he wanted a cup of coffee. He gave me a grudging nod. I mentioned how much I was looking forward to Jessica coming to live with us. "It's not a good idea," was his response. Maybe, I've been too effusive about the baby. Sometimes Jack seems to take the opposite view of things, just to be difficult. "It's the last thing we need in our lives!" he spat at me. I was shocked at the strength of his feeling. "An illegitimate child with an unknown father! Not the kind of future I hoped for my daughter!" was his next comment. Jack resents this baby; there's no doubt about it! It's not the kind of future I planned for Jessica either, but it's the only future on her horizon…mine too. We have to welcome our first grandchild into this world, I told Jack, rather than pass judgment on how the child was conceived, but he seems to have contempt for this baby, even before the birth. Maybe the joyful household of my dreams won't become reality.

I was tired and went upstairs to try to get to sleep. The sound of the television was very loud… I could hear it all the way upstairs in the bedroom. I called downstairs several times, asking if Jack would turn down the sound. He just ignored me completely. The more I kept calling down, the more he seemed determined to annoy me. When he did come upstairs, I called out, "Good night," to him. He uttered a profanity and slammed the door of his bedroom. We haven't spoken a word since. It's really hard living with Jack… I don't know if I can take any more of the mood swings. I know he's got a lot of business issues, but he doesn't need to act like this. Is this how our marriage should end up? In separate bedrooms with separate lives? We should be able to cope whenever stress or illness comes along. We should be consoling each other.

Kendra 54

I carried out Jack's wishes to set up a client event at Spelectra's box in the Verizon Center. Jack signed off on everything. I already know some of the clients. Jack has kept in touch with all his business acquaintances. I wasn't too anxious about mixing with these people. The gathering looked quite natural, simply a business invitation for clients. Even the travel arrangements stood up to scrutiny. The Tyson's office established the seating arrangements in each car. Jack took the wheel of his own car, with three other males in the car and me. I was quite relieved. This meant I didn't have to make small talk with some of the wives. We parked on the area set aside for Lexus owners at the Verizon Center. The concert was excellent. As we sat watching the performance, I felt thrilled to be in Jack's company again. Catching his eye was exciting as I wondered how the rest of the evening would progress.

Of course, Grace should have been there, but everyone knows she has MS. Nobody questioned her absence, and it didn't look too strange that she didn't attend the concert. We all decided to leave the concert before the final number since the traffic would be horrendous with the entire audience emptying out of the parking structure at the same time. After Jack dropped everyone back at Spelectra's office, we scattered back into our own vehicles. I waited to see what Jack would do. He acted just like I hoped he would. All the other cars quickly left while I made a great show of checking my purse and, apparently, making a call on my cell phone until only two cars were left in the parking lot: mine and Jack's. I waited a good five minutes to make sure the coast was clear and then walked across to Jack's car, opened the door, and sat in the passenger seat. We didn't speak at first. I put my hand over Jack's, but he didn't respond. After a few seconds, I took my hand away. We sat in silence. Then Jack grabbed my hand, entwining our fingers with a gripping intensity. After that, there was no stopping us.

When I got back to the apartment complex, I checked my appearance before getting out of the car. The well-groomed look that I presented at the concert was not reflected in the mirror. It didn't feel right going into the apartment. Su and Aidan are teenagers. They're not stupid. Just one glance would tell them what their mother had been doing. I stayed in the car until I could see that all the lights in the apartment were out and the children would be in bed. This interlude gave me time to recover some composure and think about the future. A future without Jack? That's not what I want. I want Jack in my life! My feelings for Jack are real. Grace doesn't want him anymore! Jack told me their relationship is dead. Maybe Grace would be relieved to get out of the relationship. I started to think of all the ways I could have a life with Jack instead of this clandestine affair. Does Jack love me? I don't know. Does Jack want me? There's no doubt he enjoys being with me, but how far is he prepared to go to? How far am I prepared to go?

Grace 55

I hardly slept a wink last night. My head was absolutely buzzing, but I felt good. Then it struck me. I've been having a wonderful time. I've been having so much fun that I just didn't want to go to sleep. I wanted to keep savoring every moment. I started off my week by carpooling with some friends to our favorite boutique in Georgetown. A number of little stores in the area are putting on a fashion show for one of my charities next week, so us models were due for a morning of trying on clothes for the big day. What a giggle we had in the car. We hadn't seen each other for ages, so you can just imagine all the hysteria from six grown women as we laughed at everyone's latest escapades. I'm always chosen as a model since I'm tall and skinny. Fortunately, most things look okay on me. But this time, the store manager just wasn't getting it right, so I picked out my own stuff; she doesn't know I have MS. I can't possibly stagger down the catwalk on high heels. I picked out a trendy rain coat and a jaunty little hat. I'll use an umbrella to keep me steady. It should look pretty good. Feeling hungry, we wandered farther down the street to eat lunch at Dean & Deluca on M Street. Of course, we all had a salad, not wanting to put on any weight. The chat over lunch was wide ranging—business news, cosmetics, travel stories… lots of fun. Then yesterday, I joined my garden club for a trip to Oatlands Plantation in Leesburg. It's quite an interesting house and garden tour. Afterward, we lunched at Lightfoot's. Again, the chat over lunch was such a lot of fun. I didn't want to go home. Yesterday was the annual meeting of another one of my charities, the Salisbury Foundation. All members received an impassioned e-mail pleading with us to attend since a quorum was needed for election of the new committee. So amidst the torrential rain of a spring thunderstorm, I navigated the traffic along the Beltway toward the headquarters on Connecticut Avenue. Our outgoing chair really botched up the meeting. Instead of conducting voting at the beginning of the meeting, she waited until halfway through, after a long and tedious discussion about the bylaws. By this time, a number of members voted, got thoroughly bored, and left the building. This was most unfortunate because the voting result was a tie. Not a single person knew what to do! We no longer had a quorum since half the membership had gone home. A great deal of discussion followed, and the result was we'd have to do it all over again next month. So with an unexpected date, it's just possible the rescheduled annual meeting could fail to produce a quorum yet again, and there will be a repeat performance of the whole circus.

Spelectra's results are a bit of a circus, too, way below expectations. Jack has taken the drastic step of getting rid of some of his top executives. He doesn't let it show, but I know the business situation is taking its toll on him. He's overweight, stressed, and depressed, and he's drinking heavily. He's also prone to volatile fits of anger at home. I'm sure he's not like that in the office. He just comes home and lets off steam. Unfortunately, I'm the target for the wrath that he has been bottling up all day long. My high spirits didn't last long.

Kendra 55

Schools are closing soon, so I won't have any income! The economy is improving, but companies can easily get my skills through an agency. They don't want the cost of providing benefits to permanent staff. I wonder if I can pull off a little business; maybe a coffee shop? I think it would be such fun, with lots of social contact. My friends could drop by to see me. Su and Aidan could put in a few hours. Tamara could spend time with me there instead of me having to pay for a childminder every day.

I made contact with my bank who advertize helping small business start-ups. The bank manager was very enthusiastic about setting up payroll and providing lots of other services, but he just ignores any contact from me now. Banks are so useless these days! I wonder if Jack would consider giving me a loan. My first priorities would be staff, premises, and equipment. Perhaps I'll contact the cooking school in Falls Church to see if a young graduate could shape up as a manager. I've just got to do something. I can't let my life drift along any further. I need to decide on the direction of my relationship with Jack. I need to get my accommodation situation in order. I looked at Dolley

Madison Apartments, which are quite nice. The office staff are lovely, but there's nothing available right now. Most of all, I need to work out how I'm going to get an income. It's all very confusing. I'm running out of time fast.

Maybe Jack could help me start up a little business. I could ask him for a loan. If I work hard and make a success of it, I could repay his loan quickly. I would love to make Jack proud of me! It would be so exciting to be in partnership with Jack! We could be business partners! I wonder how Jack would feel about that? He could be a sleeping partner in the business, as well as a partner in my bed! If I put my mind to it, I could take Jack away from his wife! She wouldn't suffer too badly. She would get half his income. If I set up home with Jack, that would solve all my problems. I'm just not sure if it would be morally right. Maybe my morals should take a holiday when I need a roof over my head and I have a family to feed! It just doesn't feel too good, that's all.

I'm sure I could build a new life with Jack, and we would eventually be accepted as a couple in social circles. Maybe after some years have passed, it might all settle down to feel right. I'm not sure that Jack's wife would lose too much. After all, even allowing for Grace's health issues, there must be something wrong with their marriage if he slept with me. There's no doubt that I would benefit greatly. I would enjoy the company of the man I love, I wouldn't need to work, and the children would get more attention from me and receive better fatherly guidance from Jack than they do from their biological father.

Grace 56

Well, I've been doing it for years, ever since we first moved to DC, so today, I kept my annual mammogram appointment at George Washington University Hospital. I feel very fortunate to be a patient of Dr. Brem; her mission is to eradicate breast cancer as a life-threatening disease. I used to drive to the hospital, but I can't cope with that anymore, so I took a cab to the metro at Dun Loring since the hospital is right at Foggy Bottom metro station. I took loads of reading material, but, thankfully, I was whisked straight through to the radiology department, who took the usual four images. I waited calmly, but my calm state of mind turned to concern when further images were required. After two more plates were used, I was asked to fill in a whole bunch of paperwork in preparation for an ultrasound. I started to gear myself up for bad news. I wondered why on earth I kept the routine appointment. What is the point of me being here, checking up on my health? Just a waste of time and money! A short wait and then a discussion with Dr. Brem; she placed a piece of paper on a table and asked me to sign. Feeling puzzled, I asked what else would be done today. Dr. Brem's answer was that nothing else would be done today because everything was fine. I left the building in a bit of a daze. My results are perfect. No problems at all. So many women would want to swap places with me. How could I be this lucky? My life is worth something. I do have the right to life! I made my way toward the metro station with a renewed sense of purpose. I'm not going to throw my life away! I could have another thirty years left on this earth, even though I do have multiple sclerosis. I just need to figure out where life is going to take me. I need to figure out how to make the best use of my time left on this earth.

I still need to deal with my will. I already have a notarized will that was made when the children were small, so I should revisit my wishes. I prefer not to make a song and dance over all this. Virginia law states that if a will is completely handwritten, signed, and dated, then no witnesses are required. I'm not sure if I want to discuss this with Jack; he'll just try to browbeat me into something I don't want. Maybe Miriam could witness my signature. That would reinforce the legality, I think; she could swear that I was in a sound state of mind. All my assets are in joint names with Jack, although he did get me to sign something when I was having my "episode." I can't remember what that was; he was in such a bad mood; he wouldn't give me time to read it properly.

Kendra 56

I know the man I want. I just need to work out how to make it happen. Today, I got in the car and took a little drive—right to Jack's house. I sat in the car, just down the road, and gazed at the house. If only that house was mine. My children would be all tucked up safely in bed at night with no worries. They would attend private schools, they would eat the best food, they would wear the best clothes, they would go to college, they would know the right people, and they would have a bright future. And life wouldn't be too bad for me, either. I wouldn't have to work, I would wear designer clothes, I would play golf, I would have lunch engagements every day, I would have wonderful vacations, I would drive a fancy car, and I would welcome Jack home every night to a wonderful family dinner in the dining room. I think Jack would like to have me in his house.

I watched the mail being delivered. I watched Grace walk slowly out, leaning on a cane, to collect the mail. I know Jack doesn't like going home to Grace at night. How can a vibrant man like Jack want to spend time with an invalid? If Jack and I were together, we could take active vacations—golfing, skiing, swimming, all those things. Jack could confide in me about his business problems. Grace doesn't understand. If I lived under Jack's roof, we would both be so much happier. I need to confront Jack! I need to ask him if he loves me! I need to ask him what kind of future he envisages for our relationship. But what if he gets scared? He might feel guilty thinking about a life without Grace. After all, what would everyone think? Jack doesn't live in a vacuum. He has a business to run. He has a reputation to consider. I think the thought of damaging his reputation might stop Jack from leaving Grace! After all, how good does it look that your wife becomes an invalid and you leave her for another woman? But I've got nothing to lose. Living with Jack wouldn't harm my reputation! I'm a nobody.

I just have to make Jack believe I'm special! I need him to be so madly in love with me that he doesn't care about his reputation! There's only one way I can make Jack want me so badly that nothing else matters. I have to use the same tactics that women have used ever since the beginning of time!

Grace 57

I was thinking about what I need to do with my life as I joined my art group for lunch at Katie's in Great Falls. I'm looking forward to Jessica moving in with us, but she'll go back to Boston or somewhere else after the baby is born and she finishes her MBA. Even though I want to keep the baby with us, that's not practical, Jack says. Jack is so uncomfortable about this baby. I thought he would get over his moral indignation, but his strength of feeling has increased rather than diminished. Maybe he'll change once the baby arrives; that happens in a lot of families, I think. I suppose Jack doesn't relish the thought of broken sleep and dirty diapers. I suppose he feels we'll expect him to be around a lot more, and he won't get to do what he pleases. I guess I'm expecting Jack to be the father figure for Jessica and for me. Let's face it…that's what we both need. Maybe when he sees the baby he might fall in love; that's what I'm hoping anyway. A baby should be with its mother, and Jessica needs to make a life together with her and the baby. I'll be able to enjoy an interlude with Jessica and the baby, but that will all change.

I need to think what the future holds for me. I'm involved with a lot of charities, but there's nothing too demanding…just a lot of fun, really…all hands-off stuff. One member of my art group is involved with the Salvation Army; several are members of a church. These ladies get involved directly with needy people. I wonder if I should get involved in something like that instead of all the fundraising galas and dinners Jack and I used to go to… I'm not fit for those anymore. It's hard to look the part when I'm leaning on a cane. Maybe if I found a worthwhile cause, Jack could become involved too.

Jack is in a bad mood most of the time these days. All the business pressures are getting to him. He needs to look after his health. The last thing he needs is another heart attack. I know business is not good, but he doesn't tell me anything, apart from divulging that finances are difficult and he's shed senior members of staff. I must say, I was really shocked when he told me that; this must have been a tough decision for Jack, but I guess he had no alternative. So it's no surprise that Jack is in sour spirits.

Maybe I should think of ways to cheer him up; perhaps I should make a dinner reservation. We rarely eat out together nowadays because Jack's hardly ever here. Perhaps I could do some flower arrangements to make the house look beautiful when he gets home in the evening. Of course, I could bake a cake; men always love cake, and Jack is no exception. Yes, maybe that's what I'll do… I'll bake a cake. Carrot cake would be good. In fact, I could do both… I could do a flower arrangement too. Yes, that might put Jack in a good mood…but I do feel like we need to be doing things together. What could we do?

After my escape bid, Jack has just faded into the distance. I wonder if he thinks I was just trying to get attention… I'm not sure he really believes I was trying to commit suicide. Some days I wish I had done a better job of escaping. Then I think of Jessica's baby, and there's no way I would do that again.

Kendra 57

I was giving up hope of any further assignments since the end of term is not far away, and schools organize field trips with volunteer parents to assist rather than employing substitute teachers in the classroom. I'm also giving up hope of the coffee shop idea. I mentioned it to Jack, but he didn't pass any comment. So it was a most welcome surprise when the administrator from my favorite school called yesterday to offer me a day's work. My spirits soared! Just to get out of the apartment and get my brain engaged was wonderful.

I entered the school with a big smile on my face. It was so lovely to be greeted as a familiar face. The staff smiled and said hello, and the kids waved and called out my name whenever they passed me in the hallway. At recess or in the lunchroom, the staff chat to me now as if I'm really one of the team. It's such a good feeling. Also, I can't help noticing that no one ever asks any personal questions, nobody enquires where I live or whether I have a husband and children. I'm just accepted.

Anyway, I had a terrific day with the kids. I was so impressed with their Pledge of Allegiance, the best I've ever witnessed. It was a relief to find that I had no problem students, nobody with attention deficit disorder, emotional disturbance, learning difficulties, discipline problems, or anything else. Rain had been battering down all day, so we had indoor recess. Again, the kids were simply wonderful, all quietly keeping busy and no problems at all. I knew it was too good to be true. An hour before dismissal time, an announcement came over the loudspeakers. Roads were flooded and impassable. Some school buses could not reach us. Parents would be collecting their children. Teachers would have to be prepared to stay in school for the long haul. My heart sank. What on earth would I do? Then I remembered the politician's quote: "Never waste a disaster." So I phoned Jack!

Immediately, Jack sent limousines to all three schools to pick up my family while I stayed with my class until everyone was safely home. It wasn't too late really, only six-thirty when I got out of school, but I was tired. The kids had enjoyed the excitement of sitting in Jack's huge conference room, but the novelty had worn off, and they were agitated. I put my plan into action. I invited Jack back for supper. There's always pizza in the freezer and a bottle of wine in the pantry. Jack was great with the kids, chatting to Su and Aidan and watching cartoons on TV with Tamara. I don't know what excuse he gave to Grace, but he was in no hurry to rush home. He didn't make any sign of leaving until after nine o'clock.

Jack did mention that he might have found a place for us to live. He wants me to look at apartments in McLean on the weekend. I don't quite know what Jack has in mind. He never discussed these possibilities before. As he left, I asked the kids if they would like Jack to visit again, and of course, there was a chorus of, "Yes."

Grace 58

My symptoms are worse. I'm in a bad spell. I have shooting pains from my head all the way down to my toes. My shoulders feel odd. Every time I move, there's an odd sensation there. There's a numbness on my sides, just above my hips. I have pins and needles on my feet that shoot up my leg. My knees don't seem to be working properly. I hope this will pass. I'm not eating properly, which doesn't help. I bought loads of baklava, which is in the refrigerator, so I'm making great inroads on high-calorie treats and forgetting the healthy options.

It was a great relief to enjoy the home owner's association afternoon tea today. Anything to take my mind off my symptoms. I made a special effort to look nice. I wore my navy suit with the white trimmings. I took ages over doing my hair, but it didn't look good no matter how much time I spent. There must have been fifty women there today…a good turnout. I had a lovely time catching up with many acquaintances.

I felt much better after my little outing, but, unfortunately, Jack came home in a really foul mood. I didn't expect him home early, but he had stormed out of a meeting in the office. It looks like Spelectra is on shaky ground. He said something about regulatory and policy uncertainties, as well as significant excess supply and price erosion. I don't know what that all means, but it sounds grim. So dinner wasn't ready when Jack arrived home early. I planned to make a prawn salad, but nothing was prepared. I told Jack I would start preparations straight away, but he shouted at me not to bother. Next thing I know, he's poured cereal and milk into a bowl and is sitting in front of the television. Without even looking at me, he told me to forget the salad.

I left Jack eating his bowl of cereal. I got ready for bed and went into the study to look at some documents. I wanted to check the insurance value for some of my jewelry. I also took time to look at my will… I haven't updated it yet. In the process, I found lots of outdated paperwork, so I was operating the shredding machine. In the same file as mine, Jack's will was there, so I happened to be holding it in my hand. Jack came bounding into the room and asked in a very threatening voice, "What are you doing?" When he saw me with his will in my hand and the shredding machine gobbling up paper, he seemed to think I was planning to shred his will! Why he would think I might destroy his will is incomprehensible. Clearly, he doesn't trust me! His reaction tells me I can't trust him! Jack's reaction makes me feel uneasy. I know less and less about what's going in his life; he doesn't share anything with me now, except his foul moods. He's finding more and more consolation from a bottle of vodka. I wonder if some woman is consoling him too.

Kendra 58

Another unexpected phone call from my favorite school! Only a half day's work since all the schools in Fairfax County operate short days on a Monday, but I'm never going to turn them down. The rhythm of the day feels really odd when you take the kids to lunch and then immediately back to the classroom to pack up for dismissal. While I was in the teachers' lounge, one of the full-time staff chatted to me and wanted to know how much I earn. She was horrified to discover the rate for a substitute teacher is less than a school bus driver. Anyway, it was another uneventful day with kids who were fully engaged and keen to learn. I came home feeling really relaxed and got straight into preparing dinner.

I've been thinking such a lot about Jack, so I called him to say hello. I was much more aggressive this time. Instead of waiting for him to suggest getting together, I asked when I would see him again. There was a silence at the end of the line, so I thought perhaps I had been too pushy. However, my boldness was rewarded. Jack wanted to know if I would accompany him to the Wolf Trap Ball on Saturday evening. I was absolutely thrilled at Jack's invitation! It's another client function. He explained that

Grace is not fit enough for these events anymore. She tires easily and has difficulty walking now. He thinks it's best that he has a dancing partner. I've met some of these clients before, so it won't look too odd, Jack thinks. I got much bolder as we talked. "What about afterward?" I asked. After a short pause, Jack mentioned that the Sheraton Hotel is close by and we could check in there after the event.

We had a wonderful time at the ball. Nobody gave the impression that it was uncomfortable having me at the table. I did my enthusiastic client scene of asking all about their ageing mothers, troublesome horses, and difficult teenagers. It all seemed to work really well. One of the clients remarked that I had danced my way into the event and departed in the same way. When we reached the Sheraton, I didn't hold back. Our previous liaisons have not been without shyness and embarrassment. This time, I went full throttle to give Jack a night to remember. As he left to go home to Grace, I knew I had destabilized him. I knew he would go home and never stop thinking about when we might meet again.

As we parted company, fantasies of my wedding to Jack floated in front of my eyes: just a simple ceremony in a garden in Virginia; an old manor house, perhaps; my children as witnesses; very intimate with lots of flowers; a wonderful bridal gown for me. I have to stop thinking like this. If I allow my thoughts to run away with me, there's no telling what might happen.

Grace 59

My diet is terrible. I should be focusing on all the healthy foods that would help my condition. However, everything I eat is packed with sugar. Thankfully, I'm not piling on the pounds, but only because I'm eating very little else. I need to do everything I can to avoid another episode, so my diet really needs to improve. I'm dreading another episode. I know it will happen. It could be weeks from now; it could be years from now. The uncertainty makes me anxious all the time. I need to do everything I can to avoid progressing to a wheelchair. I need to be ready for the next episode. I need to put all my affairs in order.

However, I have found a fresh purpose in life. During lunch at Katie's in Great Falls the other day, one of the ladies in my art group invited me to become a member of the Salvation Army Women's Auxiliary Guild, a wonderful organization. The Army, as it is affectionately known, started in England in the last century and is international now. Using Christian ethics, many outreach programs are underway in Washington, DC, particularly Turning Point, which provides a safe haven for single mothers while ensuring they gain an education and a position in the workplace. The whole ethos is to provide a hand up rather than a handout.

I'm so impressed with the Salvation Army that I've decided to leave a legacy. I haven't told Jack anything about it because he wouldn't agree with my sentiments. Not only that, I took Jack out of my will! My previous wishes were that he should inherit all of my estate if I die before him, but now I'm cutting him out completely. I don't even care if this doesn't stand up legally. Probably Jack could argue that we were married in community of property, but it will let him understand that I don't think him worthy of a mention. Certainly, Jessica and Edward will be significant beneficiaries, but the Salvation Army will also benefit from my death by receiving one third of my estate. Miriam has witnessed my will; it's really none of her business; she only had to sign as a witness, but she did read the contents. Miriam is the custodian of my will, and she's keeping it safely at her home. After all, Jack might shred the document if he finds it since he's obviously got that mentality!

Miriam was quite upset, telling me that I'm tempting fate by revising my will because this means I'll die soon. I've given instructions to Miriam that she needs to produce the will upon the occasion of my death. I'll tell Jessica and Edward that they should go to Miriam if anything happens to me. In the meantime, I'm looking forward to becoming involved in all the wonderful community projects at the Salvation Army.

Kendra 59

Jack called yesterday. He wasn't in a good mood because there was a code orange alert, so his golf game was canceled, and he spent the morning poring over his tax return. I was hoping he might suggest getting together, and my hopes were realized. He invited us to the Nationals Game, and I accepted with great enthusiasm. He said Grace has no interest in baseball, so it was a good opportunity to invite me and the kids to join him, along with some important clients. Being with Jack under these circumstances keeps our relationship above suspicion and gives us the opportunity to be in each other's company. However, it was not the successful day Jack planned, from a business point of view. Thankfully, the Nationals won, so everyone was pleased about that, but there was an undercurrent and a bit of a strain on the relationships because the *Washington Post* has run another critical article about Spelectra. Consequently, his clients were not in the mood to discuss business.

We drove separately to the game, and Jack met us back in the parking lot of the apartment block. As we all got out of the car, he lifted Tamara up in the air. She was squealing with delight. Just at that point, a woman smiled and waved over. Jack dropped

Tamara to the ground and scowled. As we got to the doorway, he muttered, "Let's get inside. That was one of my neighbors." Once inside, I allowed the kids to turn on the television. Jack looked tense. "That was Miriam. She'll tell Grace about seeing me with you." This was music to my ears! I don't want to hurt Grace, but I'm hoping her life with Jack is over. "I can't go on leading a double life," Jack continued. "It's stressful. I have enough stress with the business situation. I have to think about my own health. I've had enough of Grace and her health problems. I have to look after myself." I said nothing, but my impulse was to make the atmosphere feel lighthearted. I needed Jack to think that life with me would be free of the responsibility of being a caregiver. I offered to make him a margarita. He screwed up his face and declined. "Not after watching Grace at the Galleria last night." Apparently, Grace wanted to go out for a casual dinner, so they went to Sandia at the mall, where she ordered nachos and a margarita. He said just watching her picking at the nachos with her fingers and licking the salt around the glass of the margarita made him feel nauseous. I couldn't help laughing. Jack laughed too and said she was playing around with the straw and throwing her head back to make the frozen concoction slide into her mouth. At that point, he said, he wanted to throw up. We both laughed loudly as the kids turned back from the TV to see what was keeping us amused. After Jack left, I almost rubbed my hands with glee. He finds Grace nauseating! He finds me attractive! Life with Grace is stressful. Life with me is carefree. These two contrasting images in his mind are just what I need to help make him mine!

Grace 60

Out of the blue, Jack brought up the subject of our wills. He was in the library reading a book when I passed by on my way to the kitchen. He barely speaks to me when he comes home, and now, all of a sudden, he wants to discuss our wills. I do wonder what prompted this turn of events! I had plenty of stinging comments I could make, but I said nothing. He says he wants to make provision for Jessica's baby; he suggested I do the same and we should both rewrite our wills. I just raised my eyebrows and turned away. He called after me that one of his new golfing buddies has invited us to dinner so he and his wife could witness our new wills. "Oh, really! How convenient!" I answered as I moved back to the door of the library. He looked at me, with a slight smirk on his face. "Yes, it is very convenient because I've set up a blind trust." I had no idea what he was talking about. "What's that?" I asked him. "Oh, just a tax effective way of dealing with our affairs," was the reply I got. I completely saw red. "What are you doing to me?" I screamed. "I have no intention of asking total strangers to witness a legal document. I'm not going to sign something I don't understand. You're doing something fishy. I just know it." He sat there, smirking. My insides turned to jelly. I yelled and screamed. All the pent-up rage toward him just overflowed like the lava from a volcano. In mid flow, Jack snarled at me, "You're insane!" and hurled his book at me. Suddenly, my rage turned to ice. "No, you're the one who's insane," I told him coldly. "You're a complete cad!"

Well, this is the first time I've insulted Jack in all our married life. He went to bed without saying good night. He didn't even slam the door of his bedroom like he usually does. It's almost as if I had ceased to exist.

Kendra 60

Jack asked me to organize a meeting with his board members. After I had made a note of all his requirements, he told me he leased an apartment for us. I did think he was going to let me see it first, but that's just Jack. He solves all problems. He takes control.

He's also arranged for a moving company to transfer all our belongings over the weekend. I don't even need to take all my stuff out of storage since the place is fully furnished. I'm not sure why I don't feel thrilled to bits. I just have the feeling I've become a mistress. I'm beholden to Jack for a roof over my head, and I'm dependent on him for an income. The quality of my life has improved, but it feels uncomfortable. I don't want to be a hidden part of Jack's life. I don't want my children to feel obligated to a benefactor. I want to share Jack's life completely! I want to be married to Jack!

Anyway, I made reservations for the board meeting at the 1789 restaurant in Georgetown. It's not somewhere I've been before, but I checked it out, and I knew it would suit the occasion. I arranged for all the attendees to be collected from their homes in limousines. Transport is so important since traffic in Georgetown is always a major problem. The whole evening was superb. The staff was gracious and charming, and the menu was varied and beautifully presented. The décor is old town wood paneling with many interesting wall hangings, a perfect ambience for conducting delicate business. Jack tackled the major issue while dessert was served. Spelectra is in serious trouble now. The board agreed to suspend operations to evaluate reorganization options. Jack's concern was for the future of the business, but my concern was to provide the right atmosphere for the meeting. I was quietly confident that everything had proceeded as smoothly as possible, thanks to organizing just the right relaxed environment.

At the end of the evening, we were going our separate ways. As my limousine approached, the driver got out and put a bulky grocery bag into the trash can. I was alone with Jack. Jack watched the driver and commented, "What has he got in that bag? It could be body parts. Maybe he's murdered his wife and he's disposing of the body all over the city." Somehow Jack's words got me thinking some terrible thoughts. After all, what could be in that bag? Who knows, and who cares? The trash will disappear tomorrow, along with the rest of the debris from the restaurant. Awful thoughts came into my head. I started to imagine Grace's head in one of those bags. I started to think how easy it would be to dispose of her body. Trips to different trash cans all over the city would go unnoticed. The contents of the trash would also go unnoticed. If Grace was out of the picture, my relationship with Jack could develop further.

I can't stop thinking about when I'll see Jack again! He's protective toward me. He likes my company. He likes the children. The physical attraction is magnetic. Why did Jack say something like that? Just out of the blue! About someone murdering their wife!

Jack hasn't mentioned Grace for some time. I don't know what's going on there. He hasn't mentioned Jessica either. He seems to want to know more about my children than he wants to talk about Jessica and the baby. I know the plan is for Jessica to come and stay with them soon. He says Grace is ecstatic about the baby, but I think he's dreading the disruption. He did mention one of their neighbors. The one who saw us in the parking lot. He's thinks that woman will tell Grace that she saw us together. It wouldn't make me unhappy if Grace found out. In fact, it could be just what I need to push Jack over the edge. I'm feeling very confused. I have to stop thinking about what Jack said. I have to stop thinking about body parts in trash bags! I have to throw off these thoughts!

Grace 61

My heart longs for Jessica to come and live here. She tells me her long term partner has been in touch, saying that he wants to stay in her life. I'm not sure if she feels this is a good thing; it just seems to make things more complicated at this point. Jessica says that once the baby is born, she will go ahead with tests to establish if he is the father. I'm a little scared she might put the baby up for adoption if the other man is the father. Jessica hardly called before all this; now she's on the phone almost every day. I should make a wall chart and start crossing off the days. I could make a chart all covered with baby images. I'll go down to the basement tomorrow and get started on the project. Jessica and the baby will be the focus of my life from now onward. I wonder when she'll know if it's a boy or a girl… I wonder if Jessica might stay in Virginia… I'm hoping she will… I don't want her to go back to Boston.

I'm trying to forget what Miriam told me yesterday. Miriam said she was visiting her elderly aunt who stays in an apartment block in McLean. As she was parking her car, she noticed what looked like a happy family—a woman, a man, and three children. What caught her attention was the man holding a little girl in the air, who was squealing with delight. As the family walked toward the entrance, the man put his arm around the woman, hugged her, and kissed her on the cheek. She smiled over as she passed them by and was surprised to see that the man was Jack. She called over and waved, but Jack just nodded curtly. Miriam said she felt very uncomfortable telling me this. She said if Jack had introduced her to the family, it would have been fine, but since he reacted oddly, she was very troubled. I asked her to tell me when this happened. It was the day Jack was at the Nationals game. He was gone most of the day. I have no idea who this family might be. It could all be very innocent. There might be a perfectly reasonable explanation, but I have to face the facts! I never thought my husband would do such a thing, but reality is hitting me now. Jack has another woman in his life! I have to face the truth. It all adds up: the distance between us, the arguments, and the blind trust. Can it really be true? Who is this woman? And the children? How long has this been going on? Is it possible that Jack is the father of these children? Has he been leading a double life all these years? When I've been lonely and in pain, has Jack been consoling himself with this woman? Would this have happened if I didn't have multiple sclerosis? What could I have done to prevent this from happening? Is my world really crashing around me? Am I losing everything, my health and my husband? This can't be happening to me! I won't believe it unless Jack tells me himself!

I'm so thankful for Jessica and the baby. If Jack doesn't want me in his life anymore…if Jack can't cope with an invalid wife, at least I'll have my daughter and my grandchild. I won't need Jack in my life…he can go off and make a new life if he wants… I'll manage without him. After all, where has Jack been when I needed him? Does he care about me at all? Does he hate me? I don't hate him. Maybe he's not been so good at dealing with the multiple sclerosis. Even if he is seeing another woman, maybe I'm to blame…maybe if I confront him, he'll have a reasonable explanation. Even if it's true, perhaps he'll ask me to forgive him. Could I forgive him? I'll just have to hope it's not true. Miriam saw him…he can't deny that. My only hope is that Jack chooses me. But why would he do that? Why would he choose a wife who's going to be a burden for decades? What do I have to offer Jack? Why would he want to stay? I have to make him see that abandoning his wife is a poor choice. How can I do that? I need to persuade Jack that his only choice is to do the right thing; that's my only hope. I don't want to lose Jack.

Kendra 61

Last night, I met up with some girlfriends at the Greek Taverna on Old Dominion Drive in McLean. I decided to tell them all about Jack. One of my friends was shocked at my behavior. Another obviously disapproved but said nothing. She just kept looking at me and shaking her head. The other four could understand and were sympathetic because their financial situation isn't much better than mine. It's all very well to take the high ground when you don't need to worry about paying the bills or having a roof over your head. Over a few bottles of merlot, I divulged my intention to make Jack totally mine. All my friends advised that a visit to Victoria's Secret and another liaison at the Sheraton should do the trick.

Giggling like schoolgirls, we left the restaurant. I was feeling very frisky, and before I knew it, I was calling Jack on my cell phone. We agreed to meet at the Sheraton. Afterward, I told Jack I couldn't live without him. Well, it's true! I would be homeless and helpless without his protection. I told him he was the best part of my life and I couldn't bear to continue our relationship under the current circumstances. I told him he was great with the kids, who all adore him. I told him I was in love with him. All of this is really true! I'm not ensnaring him. I just told the truth. Jack said nothing. Nothing at all! All sorts of emotions flooded through me. I wanted to cry. He can't love me if he just sat there and said nothing! I went through to the bathroom and got dressed. I looked at myself in the mirror. I'm a single mother. I'm having an affair with a married man. This man's wife is an invalid. What have I been doing? I've been pinning all my hopes on Jack. I'm just a convenient consolation to him, that's all. Imagining myself as Jack's wife! What a fool! If I had the courage, I would tell Jack I have to end the relationship because there's no future for us. That would be one way of pushing him to make a choice. But I can't take that risk. I wanted to tell him I would move out of the new apartment as soon as I could find a proper place for my children to live as a family, rather than some transient misfits in an anonymous high rise building. But beggars can't be choosers! Jack has provided a roof over our heads. I can't throw that in his face and walk out! Even if he doesn't love me, I do love him. I'll take the crumbs from his table! As I opened the door of the hotel room, I looked back. Jack was sitting motionless on the bed, staring into space.

Grace 62

Jessica paid an unexpected weekend visit; she called to say she would arrive on Friday and wanted to spend Saturday with me...a girl's day out. Edward joined us for dinner on Friday evening. So happy to see that boy; as usual, he brought a thoughtful gift...a little purse to wear around my waist so that my balance won't be affected by carrying a handbag. He's so helpful when he visits...always asks what he can do for me. Anyway, Jessica made coffee after dinner and then said she had something to show us. A scan. A scan of the baby. It's a girl! Now we can all imagine this child in our lives. My thoughts were racing ahead, thinking of all the cute things I can buy for this baby girl, imagining her first day at school... I can't wait to hold her in my arms.

Jack wasn't at home to hear Jessica's news. He's been gone since I confronted him about the mystery woman. It turns out that Kendra was the woman in the parking lot. What a fool I've been! It was so obvious all along. He never had anything but praise for her, right from the minute she first came into his life...so hard working...such a positive attitude...such a good mother...what a wonderful sense of humor...that was Kendra. I should have heard the warning bells long ago. But I trusted Jack. I could never imagine that he would be unfaithful to me. Multiple sclerosis changed everything! I was always bright and lively…that's the person Jack knew and loved…that's the person who could meet Jack's needs. I've become a shrunken shell. That's not what Jack needs in his life. He looked ashamed when I confronted him. "Who is she?" I asked. He sighed and muttered her name. I think he was waiting for a tongue lashing… I certainly had one prepared in my head. I also had another approach to use. I didn't make it easy for him. If I had shouted and screamed, he would have simply walked out. When he used her name… I used silence. I let that empty space fill up with my imaginings of them together, hoping that guilt would enter his soul. The silence was endless. Eventually, I heard the words I wanted to hear. "I'm sorry." I wanted to scream at him, "Sorry for what?" I stayed silent. What is he sorry about? Sorry he got found out? Sorry I have multiple sclerosis? Sorry about Jessica's baby? Sorry he's been unfaithful, or sorry he hasn't been here for me? Or is he saying sorry for what the future will hold?

Kendra 62

I knew if I called Jack he would want to see me again, but, above all, I needed him to call me! Two days passed. I decided I couldn't leave it any longer. I would swallow my pride and accept my role as Jack's mistress, even though that means being a home wrecker. That's what I am, but I can't help it. I love Jack. Just before ten o'clock at night, the phone rang. Jack's voice! He asked me to accompany him to Philadelphia on a business trip. He called me as if nothing has happened.

I made my own travel arrangements. The Tyson's office dealt with Jack's travel plans. We arranged to meet in the foyer lounge of the Downtown Marriott on Filbert Street to discuss the days ahead. Jack ordered coffee while I got my notebook out, ready for instructions. I looked him right in the eye, with my pen poised. "I love you," he said. I wasn't sure if he really said that or if it was just a voice in my head. I closed my eyes. All the bruising around my heart stopped hurting. I looked up to the ceiling as relief flooded through me. I just won the heart of the man I love! I wanted to jump up and down. A huge grin broke out all over my face! I felt really goofy! I could barely look into his eyes in case it wasn't true.

But there was a light in Jack's eyes I had never seen before...he had given his heart to me.

I was the most efficient executive assistant Jack ever encountered on Thursday and Friday. On Saturday, we had one meeting in the conference room of the hotel, and the rest of the day was free. Jack suggested some sightseeing, so we wandered around Reading Market and then made our way to the Liberty Bell and the Constitution Center. At the end of the day, we enjoyed relaxing over pasta and a bottle of wine at Maggiano's, opposite the hotel. As Jack took out his wallet to pay the bill, he handed me three envelopes. "Choose one," he said as he gave his credit card to the server.

Clearly, Grace was deranged when she wrote those suicide notes. "Who knows about these?" I asked. "No one. No one but you." My first thought was how different my life would be right now if Grace had accomplished what she intended! My second thought was wondering why Jack was showing these to me. I looked at him questioningly.

"Choose one," he said again. I folded two letters back into their envelopes and set them on the table at Jack's elbow. I read the last letter again, returned it to the envelope, and handed it to Jack. He put two envelopes in the side pocket of his jacket and one into his wallet. I watched, with a pounding heart, as the envelope joined the other aspects of Jack's life, hiding beside credit cards and banknotes, each item with an uncertain future.

I couldn't understand why Jack was showing me those letters. I was even more mystified that he asked me to choose one. He didn't explain, and it seemed better not to ask. If Grace *had* taken her own life, would I still have a relationship with Jack? He would be consumed with all the aftermath. Perhaps we would never have strayed into an intimate relationship. Or maybe he would have felt released from his obligations and free to enter a relationship with me that didn't need to be clandestine. I did venture one question. "What if she had done it, Jack? What would that have meant for us?"

Grace 63

I don't know how I found the strength to carry on. When Jessica called to say she was home from a business trip, I was so relieved; her next phone call drained the blood from my veins. "Mom, I've got something to tell you." I just knew I didn't want to hear what she would say next. Those words "I lost the baby" stung every fiber of my being. Jessica's problem is solved, I suppose is the only positive way to view the situation; that's her father's view, but I don't think I'll ever see it that way. Jessica is not a young woman. She's thirty-one years old; the only man in her life was a reluctant father, and he's melted away, she tells me. So maybe Jessica's problem is solved, but I'm grieving—not just for the loss of the baby but for Jessica's future…and my future, too. I was so looking forward to having Jessica come and live here, the excitement of a new baby in the house, having Jessica's company—so much has gone. It's been a week of bad news. In fact, I don't remember a week quite like this. Jessica phoned a few days later to tell me she would still spend time in Virginia doing her MBA, but she has taken a lease on an apartment in McLean, a brand new place, Halstead Square; she says she's very impressed with the security arrangements, which is so important for a woman living alone. She said all kinds of people live there…young couples with babies in strollers, as well as older children and single men. "Maybe I'll meet a nice man there, Mom," was her attempt to console me. What did surprise me was she mentioned bumping into Kendra. "She's living there?" I questioned. "Surprised me too," Jessica acknowledged. "It's a little above her price range."

After Jessica's news, I didn't much care about anything. I'm still trying to come to terms with Jack's latest news. Spelectra needs to evaluate its options, he said, which includes filing for bankruptcy under Chapter 11. The house will have to be sold… I have to move to a smaller place…maybe a condo or an apartment…a lot less maintenance and no stairs for me. It's something that would be coming down the tracks anyway, he said, and means I'll have less to worry about. I always suspected this business venture would be a disaster! All we've sacrificed all these years, all our savings and all our memories, all gone down the drain! Our relationship is down the drain too! My husband of twenty-five years chose his mistress over me, and he can't provide for me in my old age! I don't trust Jack anymore! I've lost my husband and my grandchild. Now I'm losing my house as well as my health. A tiny little apartment…that's okay for Jessica, but I've got a house full of memories here, memories of happy times with Jack and memories of the children growing up. I won't have Miriam next door. All my stuff will have to go; you can't put a house full of possessions into an apartment. My beautiful antique furniture will have to go… I have no idea how I'm going to cope with all of this. Then I got my first taste of revenge. "How about those new apartments on Gallows Road? Halstead Square? Jessica just told me she's moving in there. I could live there too!" Jack looked like I had punched him in the stomach. He shook his head and walked away.

Kendra 63

I was surprised when Jack suggested I accompany him on a long weekend to New York! I thought he wouldn't need me for any more assignments. Spelectra is in trouble, he told me, and he doesn't think the company will survive, but he says his personal wealth won't be affected. He'll actually come out of all this in a better financial position than when he started! Both of us were in a buoyant mood when we boarded the Acela from Union Station on Friday evening and checked into the Ritz Carlton in Downtown Manhattan. Jack's meeting wasn't until Monday, so we took advantage of the time to unwind. We were just steps away from the ferry to Ellis Island and the Statue of Liberty, so it was a good opportunity for sightseeing on Saturday.

In the evening, Jack managed to get tickets for *Wicked* on Broadway by paying double the face value to the concierge at the hotel. On Sunday, we kept the "Do not Disturb" sign outside our room. The only time we opened the door was to allow room service to deliver omelets and champagne. On Monday morning, Jack had to meet with his bankers. All went well, and he left smiling broadly, with handshakes all round. As our cab sped through the financial district on the way back to the hotel, Jack suddenly ordered the driver to stop. He pulled me out of the car into the sparkling entrance of Tiffany's, with instructions to choose anything on display. I was stunned and couldn't think straight. After all, did he mean a necklace or a ring—a pretty significant difference. Jack led me toward a case containing rings as well as necklaces. "Choose a ring," he commanded. I felt like Cinderella as I chose the one that fitted best!

Kendra 64

After the meeting with the bankers on Monday, and visiting Tiffany's, we returned to the hotel with one thing on our minds. The bed sheets were very rumpled by mid afternoon! We enjoyed an early dinner at a nearby restaurant before returning to the hotel for an early night, ready for the journey back to Virginia in the morning. Jack couldn't sleep. He tossed and turned. Eventually, he pulled on some clothes and said he was making his way to the bar for a drink. It was just after ten o'clock. When the door closed, I wondered whether to follow him, but the only thing I felt like doing was admiring my new solitaire. It's just fabulous! I never thought I would be displaying such a rock on my finger! An hour passed. Two hours passed. I was feeling anxious, but didn't want to get all dressed just to go down to the bar. Neither did I relish welcoming Jack back into my bed if he was drunk! After three hours I was worried. What should I do? Call his cell phone? But then he wouldn't appreciate me acting like a nagging wife! I woke up at six in the morning. No Jack! He had been gone for almost eight hours! My stomach lurched. My eyes roved the room, searching for inspiration. Jack's briefcase was there; his suit was there; his shoes were there. The only thing missing was Jack and the casual clothes he had pulled on to go down to the bar. I rummaged through Jack's briefcase to see if he had taken his cell phone. Maybe I should call him now.

My hands touched the envelopes containing Grace's suicide notes. A shiver went down my spine, as I read them again. But there were only two! One of the suicide notes was missing! A folder caught my eye. The name of Spelectra's law firm was emblazoned on the front. I dared to look at the contents. A bunch of documents all related to a trust. A trust, naming the beneficiaries as me and the children! A flimsy piece of paper was stuffed into one of the zip pockets. A car rental agreement! Jack rented a car in New York. That surprised me, because I made all the travel arrangements for the trip. He must have organized the car rental through the concierge. I understood we were returning to Virginia the same way we came—by train. It's a long car drive, over four hours. I decided to take a shower and get dressed, before figuring out what to do next. I was pacing the floor, giving it just ten more minutes before calling Jack's cell phone. I rushed over to the bedside, as the unfamiliar tones of the hotel landline shot fear into my heart. It was Jack! "You awake, honey? Come on down for breakfast." Ten hours since Jack disappeared down to the cocktail bar! I was dreading sitting at a breakfast table with Jack nursing a hangover. He did sound very odd on the phone. However, I found him in a very up-beat mood. He said he couldn't sleep, last night, with all the excitement from yesterday. He said he went for a walk and found a bar, down the street from the hotel, and had a couple of drinks. After that he just kept walking around, his thoughts racing about our future together. He didn't want to disturb me. He talked loudly and laughed a lot over breakfast. He created lots of banter with the servers in the restaurant. I've never seen this side of Jack before! Jack is usually low key and doesn't want to attract attention. I felt a little conspicuous with guests at nearby tables looking across at us. But then I decided to give them something to look at. Drumming my fingers on the table soon caught their attention, as the new diamond on my finger sparkled under the chandelier. "Let's go, honey" Jack called out to me, "We don't want to miss that train".

Kendra 65

Jack returned to Virginia to find that Grace had disappeared! A suicide note on the kitchen table was confirmation that Grace had taken her own life. The reasons were obvious. Grace had nothing to live for, anymore. Multiple sclerosis, the loss of her unborn granddaughter, and the failure of Spelectra left her with no reason to live. Grace was angry and resentful at having to move out of the family home. Jack told the police that she became hysterical about moving to a smaller place, threatening to kill herself, on more than one occasion. Such a selfish woman! She never experienced one day of financial hardship in her life. I wonder how she would have coped with trying to survive under my circumstances!

Everyone who had contact with Grace, during the last twenty four hours of her life has been interviewed by the police. No-one can throw any light on how Grace met her death. The body has not been discovered but, on the basis of the handwritten note, the police have concluded that Grace did commit suicide. The investigation remains open.

Jack has been very stressed throughout this whole situation. All the dealings with the police and the life insurance company have been exhausting. Fortunately, Jack sheltered his investment in Spelectra, so his personal finances are unaffected by the failure of the company. It will be a huge bonus if the life insurance pays out.

Jack wants us to get married in Las Vegas, once the aftermath of Grace's death has died down, but I feel increasingly uncomfortable about her disappearance. How long do we have to wait before she is classified as dead? What if she suddenly turns up?

Kendra 66

I'm haunted by Grace. Where is she? What happened to her? I don't want to face the possibility that Jack... the night she disappeared. The police interviewed me. They wanted confirmation that Jack was in New York that night. I told them...yes...we traveled together to New York by train...we shared a hotel room...yes...we traveled back by train.

I haven't seen much of Jack since our trip to New York. There's been so much for him to deal with. Somehow, the excitement of getting together has disappeared along with Grace! Jack seems different to me now. Somehow there's a hollow feeling in the pit of my stomach. He was gone from the hotel room for ten hours! Where did he go? Why did he rent a car? What did he do? I don't know! I don't know!

Last night, after the kids were in bed, I was sitting at the kitchen table trying to figure it all out. What if I went to the police to tell them that Jack went missing that night? What if they knew there were three suicide notes? What if I don't tell the police? I think I could be in trouble. I think withholding information might be a crime!

What has happened to Grace? It will all come out, some day...maybe tomorrow...maybe next year...maybe in ten years time. Where will I be when the truth comes out? Married to Jack? What would happen then? If Jack was involved...where would that leave me? What would happen to me? Would I be an accessory to a crime?

Kendra 67

I couldn't sleep last night...again...it's been like that since Grace disappeared. The white leather sofa in the new apartment has witnessed me staring into space for many nights now...my hand strokes the smooth surface...seeking comfort. Light catches the facets of my solitaire, shooting off dazzling rays in every direction. I'm so in love with that fabulous diamond. I can admire it for hours on end. It means everything to me. It means someone loves me. It means I'm financially secure. That's all I want, really. But I don't feel secure. A growing sense of unease is creeping into my world.

I really thought sheltering under the wing of a successful man would make all my dreams come true. I thought that would make me happy. All my problems would be solved. But I don't feel happy. I feel empty. There should be laughter in my life... lighthearted laughter...like I don't have a care in the world.

I keep telling the kids that life is about making the right choices. Poor choices have bad consequences. I've made poor choices in my life. Is this another one? Complete dependence on a man? What kind of man? Do I really know this man?

I've started thinking. I could accept that position at the school. I turned it down when they offered it to me. I didn't give a reason…just said things were up in the air. I know it's still open…a nice school…a permanent position. Back to a life of scrimping and scraping…just when all my worries seem to have vanished? Could I cope with that? There's lots of upsides…health care for me and the kids…and I would be independent. I could use the last of my nest egg. I could become a certified teacher in just twelve months. Maybe I could even become a school principal. I love working with kids. I could struggle along…just like always…without a man in my life.

Kendra 68

They found her on the banks of the Potomac in Great Falls Park. Some hikers found her body washed up on the shore early one morning. I feel as if she's haunting me…like she's watching me…every move I make. She's on my mind all the time…whatever I'm doing…Grace is filtering through. I try to block her out…but she's accusing me…not saying anything… just this spooky aura…like she's going to take over my life…like she's never going to go away…it gets more intense every day. I want to shake her off…but she's always there…it feels like she's trying to invade my life…steal my energy from me… I suppose I did steal her husband from her. Is that what she's doing…seeking revenge from the grave?

The police have interviewed Jack again, he told me. I'm really scared now. They'll want to talk to me again, I'm sure. What would happen if Jack gets accused of something? He would go to prison. Maybe he would face execution; that would mean I would be a beneficiary of the trust for me and the children. I have to think straight.

I can't live like this…anxiety every day…the only person who can take this away is me. I don't want blood money…Grace's blood money! My dream is turning into a nightmare!

Kendra 69

I called the hotel in New York. I asked the concierge to fax me a copy of the car rental. Over five hundred miles on the clock...the night Grace disappeared! The night Jack told me he was in a bar drinking and walking around the streets of New York!

I should tell the police about the car rental... Jack never mentioned it to me. My nightmare is turning into reality! Did Jack drive all the way to Virginia and back to New York on the night Grace went missing? If there's any suspicion, I'll be escaping from a bad situation. If there's a reasonable explanation for the car rental, I'll be the happiest woman alive! I can't live in fear and dread! I have to have hope in my heart!

I'm scared. I hope I have the courage to do the right thing! Tomorrow morning, I'll call the police...but...maybe, I'll lose my resolve in the morning. There's no point in waiting. I might lose my nerve in the morning. There's no reason to wait. I'll call them now. No more poor choices!